CORPSE MOUNTAIN

ANDERSEN PRUNTY

GRINDHOUSE PRESS

Corpse Mountain (formerly titled *Slag Attack*)
Grindhouse Press #107
grindhousepress.com
Paperback ISBN: 978-1-957504-22-3
Copyright © 2010 and 2024 by Andersen Prunty
notandersenprunty.com
Cover design copyright © 2024 by Andersen Prunty
Front cover image by Ralwell/Shutterstock.com
Front cover background vector by Zack C/Shutterstock.com

CORPSE MOUNTAIN

Also by Andersen Prunty

<u>Novels & Novellas</u>

Meat Photo (with C.V. Hunt)
Dreaditation
Neon Dies At Dawn
Irrationalia
Failure As a Way of Life
This Town Needs a Monster
Squirm With Me
Sociopaths In Love
The Warm Glow of Happy Homes
Satanic Summer
Fill the Grand Canyon and Live Forever
Fuckness
The Sorrow King
Morning is Dead
My Fake War
The Beard
Zerostrata
Jack and Mr. Grin

<u>Collections</u>

Bodies Wrapped in Plastic and Other Items of Interest
Deathtripping: Collected Horror Stories
Creep House: Horror Stories
Bury the Children in the Yard: Horror Stories
Pray You Die Alone: Horror Stories
Sunruined: Horror Stories
The Driver's Guide to Hitting Pedestrians
Hi I'm a Social Disease: Horror Stories
The Overwhelming Urge

CONTENTS

PART ONE
THE DEVASTATED INSIDES OF HOLLOW CITY
1

PART TWO
VINCENT SEVERITY
33

PART THREE
CORPSE MOUNTAIN
55

PART FOUR
ALL ALONE AT THE EDGE OF THE WORLD
77

PART ONE

THE DEVASTATED INSIDES OF HOLLOW CITY

1

In the flickering bathroom light, Shell adjusts his eyepatch and runs a hand across the black scruff of his jaw before vomiting into the sink. He glances at himself in the mirror, a single cold blue eye glaring back at him, surrounded by a hundred and forty pounds of waste. He dips his fingertips into the puke, moving it around, looking for signs of infection.

He breathes a sigh of relief at the absence of the tell-tale maggot-like worms. *Was* it relief? Perhaps.

He coughs and turns the tap on cold. He catches the water in his hands and splashes it on his face, trying to get the puke smell off his upper lip.

The flickering light irritates him. He reaches up to either tighten or unscrew the bulb altogether and notices it's covered in thick, slug-like worms. Adult slags. He can't bring himself to touch them.

The Rotting Man never told him this city was infested.

But Shell isn't here because of the infestation. He's here for a different reason. That reason is, as yet, unbeknownst to him.

He checks his watch. Two more hours until The Rotting Man will call. Maybe he has enough time for a nap.

2

His tiny room consists of a bed and desk. The door opens outward, banging into the far wall of the narrow hall and there it is. His bed. A single bed. No floor space. The small desk sits atop the bed. The desk has a chair but in order to lie down in the bed he has to put the chair on top of the desk before crawling beneath it. It's the worst room in the world.

He pulls all the covers from the bed, making sure there are no slags on it. He doesn't really need the covers anyway. It's nearly a hundred degrees and humid. Summer in Hollow City. He's already damp with sweat.

Lying in bed, he listens to distant sirens, trains and, closer, insects. They sound frenzied. As much a victim of the slags as humans. He falls asleep only briefly and dreams of torture and explosions. In the dream, he's another person entirely but everyone pretends to know him and, for some reason, this makes him violently angry.

He awakes to the desperate blatting of his cell phone. He looks at it. A picture of The Rotting Man, drunk, greets him. The picture was taken at last year's Christmas party. The Rotting Man had drunk way too much and kept asking people if they wanted to go out and roll winos at the train station. That was just before The Rotting Man's left ear fell off.

Good times? Doubtfully.

Shell flips his phone open.

"Yeah."

"You asleep?"

"It's like six in the evening. Why the hell would I be asleep?"

"Different strokes for different folks!"

"Is everything you say a fucking cliché?"

"Find Pearl. That's all I got for you. And that's no cliché."

"Who's Pearl?"

"Find her. Do what you do best." Another cliché.

"I don't suppose I'll get any help with this one?"

"Help is all around you, friend . . ."

"Okay. Gotta go." Talking to The Rotting Man is headache inducing. There's only so much of it he can take, and because of the clichés, Shell can almost predict how he'll answer his questions. So why even bother asking them?

There is an awkward pause. Shell holds the phone away from his ear to see if the call has ended. The seconds continue to roll on the tiny screen.

"Say it!" The Rotting Man blurts.

Shell takes a deep breath and says, "See you later alligator," in his customary monotone.

"After while crocodile!" The Rotting Man gleefully yells back before ending the call.

3

Shell slides out of bed, which means he's now standing in the hallway.

Help is all around you. Is that a cliché? Shell isn't sure. He thinks it sounds like a cliché. Whatever. Most of what The Rotting Man says is bullshit anyway. But he's the boss.

Shell straightens his tie and grabs his coat from the chair, pulling it on and smoothing out the wrinkles. It's what his ex-wife disdainfully calls "detective brown." He again touches his eyepatch, a weal of nausea streaking across his insides.

He walks down the short and narrow hallway until he comes to the dim living room. Miss Fitch, an older lady mostly made of bones and hair, is on her knees. Her arms are clasped around the flickering television. Her cheek is pressed against the glass and she's crying loudly. Gushing. The static has captured her hair and spread it across the television. From what Shell can tell it's just a harmless sitcom. At first he thought it might be more of the plague footage: mountains of dead, slag-gnawed children, skinny three-legged dogs wandering through it all, cities abandoned and destroyed. He stands and stares at her. Earlier, she had been sitting on the couch, her hands demurely folded in her lap while she stared catatonically at the wall.

The landlord, a fat hirsute hunchback named Mr. Blatz, had warned Shell about her. "She came with the building," he had said. "She's always been here." Then he had offered to knock ten dollars off the rent. That sounded good to Shell. He wouldn't need the apartment much more than a night, anyway.

Between the sobs, Miss Fitch bellows, "Stop looking at me!" Flecks of spittle hit the screen, pixilating it. "Oh God, just quit looking at me."

Shell clears his throat. "I've gotta go in the kitchen and make some calls. Do you think you can keep the crying to a minimum?" He holds the thumb and forefinger of his right hand very close together.

She is once again wracked with sobs. "Oh God, now it's *talking* to me."

Who is *she* talking to?

"I'll have you know," Shell begins. "I am not an 'it'. I am a man. Living. Breathing. Human."

She pulls away from the screen to face him, her teeth bared. She snarls, "Hollow. You're all hollow!"

Shell can't take her seriously. Half her hair is still plastered to the television. He remembers what Mr. Blatz said about trying not to instigate her but he can't seem to help it.

"I'd think a resident of Hollow City wouldn't be so quick to make that judgment."

But she's turned back to the television, rubbing her cheek up and down it. On the screen, a fat man in a red bra laughs uproariously as someone sprays him with a garden hose. "Please," she whispers. "Just make him go away."

"As I said," Shell crosses the living room, giving Miss Fitch a wide berth. "I was just going into the kitchen to make some calls. I'd rather not be bothered."

But she's gone, licking the television and rubbing her nose in the saliva. Shell looks for slag movement in the saliva but doesn't see anything. He makes his way into the overly bright kitchen. A large sullen man in overalls sits at the table and stares at a plate of runny scrambled eggs.

Shell turns back to the living room to address Miss Fitch. "Say, do you know who Pearl is?"

Slowly, she pulls her glistening face from the screen and pushes a button, turning the television off and plunging the living room into darkness. Her eyes have once again gone blank. She slumps over to the couch and plops down.

"Pearl?" he asks and knows he will not get a response.

4

Shell approaches the man sitting at the table.

"Mr. Blatz didn't say anything about you."

The man says nothing.

"That means I don't really have to let you stay. Normally, I wouldn't mind. You seem quiet and I won't be here long. But I need some privacy. I have some calls to make and that room . . ." he gestures toward his room, "is far too small and hot to think."

The man makes no attempt to leave. Shell picks up a handful of the eggs and shoves them into the bib of the man's overalls.

"Just take your eggs and go."

The man pats his egg-filled pouch, slides his chair back from the table and stands. "You'll be sorry," he says softly and slowly.

"Do you know who Pearl is?" Shell asks.

"I wouldn't tell you if I did. You're very rude."

Then, in a half-hearted attempt at confrontation, the man flips his plate over onto the table, the remaining eggs slathering across the surface.

"Dick," Shell says.

"Monster," the man says softly, lethargically pushing Shell's shoulder.

"I don't want to fight you."

"You'd lose anyway." The man lumbers to the door, turns back and says, "I hope you fail."

"I probably will," Shell says and thinks, *I almost always do.*

He finds the best way to thoroughly insinuate himself into a city is to use a local landline and call local people. The phone is mounted to a wall and covered in slags. He grabs the dirty plate from the table and attempts to knock the writhing slags from the phone. They fall to the floor with wettish plops. He stomps them. This is really the perfect size to combat them. Not large enough to make a giant mess but not small enough to go undetected. The baby ones could be anywhere. Even inside you. Before you know it they're all over and all hope is lost.

He picks up the phone and calls a random number.

"Hello," a male voice says.

Calling someone is like putting himself right in their house. He can hear if they are watching television. He can hear if they have a dog or children. If they're eating. This guy doesn't seem to be doing anything. It's easy to imagine him just sitting by the phone and staring out into nowhere.

"Hi," Shell says. "Um, what are you wearing?" He feels this is a good opening line. Sometimes people hang up on him but there are always plenty more numbers to call.

"Well," the man says. "I'm wearing pants and a shirt."

"What about shoes? Are you wearing shoes?"

"Yep."

"What kind?"

"Brown work boots."

"What about socks?"

"Yep."

"Ankle, crew, or tube?"

"Um, well, I guess they's ankle socks."

"What kind of pants are you wearing?"

"Just jeans."

"Blue?"

"As the sky."

"What about your shirt? What kind of shirt are you wearing?"

"It's a t-shirt. And, well, I'm ashamed to say this but . . . it's kind of pink. It used to be red but it's faded a lot."

"Can you tell me about Pearl?"

"Pearl?"

"Yeah. Pearl."

"No. I'm afraid I can't."

"Do you know her?"

"Oh, everybody knows Pearl. She's the Queen of Town."

"The Queen of Town?"

"Well, of Hollow City anyway."

"What does she look like?"

"Do I know you?"

"Yeah, definitely. I'm Mike from down the street."

"Well, if anyone knows what Pearl looks like then I would think it should be you. Wanna do me a favor? Stop yankin' my cock. Bye."

"Wait."

"Bye."

Shell doesn't hang up the phone. He waits until he knows the other person is gone. But this guy doesn't seem to hang up either.

"Are you still there, Mike?"

Shell doesn't know who the man is talking to until he remembers that he's Mike.

"Still here. Are you ready to tell me yet?"

"I just say you should know 'cause you was the last person to see her."

Suddenly, Shell feels confused, like the man is accusing him of something. He bangs the phone down in its cradle on the wall and takes a deep breath. Miss Fitch has worked her way out of the living room and is dragging herself into the kitchen by her arms, her legs trailing out behind her. Shell wonders why she does this since he just saw her walk only moments before. He has to get out of the apartment. He opens the door, slams it behind him and walks briskly out into the hallway, down the stairs and outside.

The city isn't anything like it was when he went in.

5

When he had first arrived, the area surrounding the apartment building had been just like any other slightly rundown Main Street of a small city. Stately trees stood by the side of the road. Children played in yards. People sat on the porches of their large, old houses.

Now it is a flurry of noise and activity.

A squad of at least four helicopters, maybe news choppers, maybe police choppers, swoop low over the houses, scouring the early evening streets and alleys. It seems like everyone is outside, yelling and pointing. They parade up and down the streets, most of them looking furious and ready for a fight. The doors of many houses have been flung open, furniture and other debris flying out the door to land in porches and yards. The children have formed two large packs, now engaging in a rumble in a vacant lot at the corner. A young woman wields a chainsaw and cuts down a tree by the side of the road. The tree falls out into the road, smashing cars parked along the curb, and she ritualistically moves on to the next one. A car speeds down the road until it slams into the downed tree. Rather than driving around the tree the driver continues forward in an attempt to drive over it. The front wheels squeal over the tree in a smoky grind of burning wood and rubber until both sets of tires are suspended, spinning around and around in midair. The driver, furious, gets out of the car, slams the door and levels several vicious kicks at it until there is a very visible dent. Then he flings his arms up into the air and collapses into a screaming heap amidst the leaves fanned out on the asphalt.

Standing in the parking lot of the building, Shell wonders what he will find if he ventures forward. The man in overalls stands to his right plucking scrambled eggs out of his overalls and eating them. He looks at Shell. Fear, or something, twists his facial features and he collapses to the ground on all fours. He heaves out the eggs onto the asphalt. Shell doesn't feel so well himself. He clutches his stomach and vomits next to the man. Crouching down, he once again sees that his vomit is clear of infection. The same cannot be said for the man in overalls. His puke crawls with baby slags. Enough to make it look alive. And a smell, something Shell equates with death, wafts up and hangs around both men. The man rises and wipes the back of his hand against his mouth. Shell takes a cautious step back from him.

Apparently their vomiting together has forged some sort of solidarity.

"It's okay to laugh at me," the man says. "I know I'm dying."

Shell surveys the destruction, the fervid activity all around him, and realizes he has many questions but only one that really matters.

"I'm sorry you're dying," he says to the man. "I wish I could help you but I have to find Pearl. Do you even know who Pearl is?"

"She's the Queen of Town."

Shell watches the man's puddle of vomit as the slags disperse outward from it, making it look like the puddle is growing.

"I've heard that. Do you know what she looks like?"

"She looks like a Queen. Only she's very small. Young. Like eight."

"An eight-year-old is your Queen?"

"Stranger things have happened. She doesn't control everything . . ." He takes a deep breath. "Just the stuff that matters."

Shell gestures at the chaos around him. "I would have thought she controlled everything judging by the way her absence has allowed complete and total anarchy."

"Anarchy?" the man says. "This isn't anarchy. These people are all trying to find Pearl. They want to bring her back from wherever she is. If it were anarchy then it would be like it was before Pearl and I don't . . . I don't even want to think of that. I'd love to stay and chat but I have to join the search. Everyone is looking for her."

"Say, you wouldn't happen to know anyone named 'Mike,' would you?"

"I know a lot of Mikes."

"Is your name Mike?"

"I have to go."

With that, the man in overalls walks out amidst the chaos.

Where to begin? Shell thinks.

6

He doesn't even have any transportation. What does The Rotting Man actually expect him to do? He sends him to a town to look for someone the whole town is already looking for. What makes The Rotting Man think he'll be any luckier? This is not the standard case.

The Rotting Man didn't even mention a commission and Shell, so flustered with his environment, didn't think to ask. Usually he found himself looking for people who everyone else had given up looking for. In this day of the slags and the plague it was easy for state and local authorities (those that still existed, anyway) to write people off. The common belief was that people became infected with the slags and then crawled out into the woods or the bowels of some huge city to die. For the person to be found, this could be a good or a bad thing.

Shell never knows if he is demon or angel. The Rotting Man tells him who to find. Shell sometimes finds that person and presents them to The Rotting Man. The Rotting Man gives him a certain sum, depending on the person. What happens to the person, Shell does not know. Nor does he particularly care. To borrow come clichés from The Rotting Man: A paycheck is a paycheck and business is business. Those clichés have not changed since the infestation.

According to the man on the phone, the last person to be seen with Pearl was a man named Mike. Of course, if Pearl was "like eight," how old would the last person to be seen with her be? Shell doesn't think he sounds like an eight-year-old on the phone but, given other strange behaviors he's witnessed, he doesn't think he can rely too much on logic. For that matter, he can't even be sure the man on the phone was telling the truth. Shell generally assumes everyone he speaks to is a liar, whether they know it or not. Most people are living lies, Shell thinks. They live those lies until they believe them and then they take them to the grave. Maybe, if there is any justice in the cosmic universe, the truth is known in death.

Stepping onto the sidewalk, Shell approaches the woman wielding the chainsaw. She furiously saws away at a large maple tree, sawdust covering her ankle-length dress and caught up in her brown hair, a frantic look in her eyes, her jaw tense.

"Excuse me," Shell says.

She pulls the chainsaw away from the tree, not turning it off, and eyes Shell. "What do *you* want?"

"I just wanted to ask why you were sawing down all these trees."

"Isn't it obvious?"

"If it were obvious I probably wouldn't be asking."

"I'm looking for *Pearl*. You know *Pearl*, don't you?"

"I've heard of her but I don't really know that much about her." It's his common routine to act as ignorant to any given situation as he can. People usually want to inform the uninformed. "For instance, why would she be hiding in a tree?"

"Boy, you really are dense, aren't you?"

"I'm not incredibly bright, no."

"Trees make excellent hiding spots."

"Like up in the tree?"

"Like *in* the tree, smartass."

Shell looks at the tree. "I still . . . I guess I still don't understand. How could she be *in* the tree?"

"She could hollow it out and crawl right in there. This is Hollow City. It got that name for a reason, okay? Like not everything has an inside. Some of it's just emptiness. And if I find one of the hollow trees then I can almost assure you I'll find Pearl."

"So how long has Pearl been missing?"

"Look, don't you read the paper? I don't have time to stand here and answer any more of your stupid questions."

She revs the chainsaw and begins sawing at the tree again. Shell wants to ask her how she knows she won't just cut Pearl in half if she *is* hiding in a tree but thinks better of it. One does not goad the frenzied bearers of chainsaws.

The sky grows darker. Soon it will be twilight and then evening. Shell doesn't want to think what this place is like after dark. A frumpy middle-aged woman throws open the front door of her house, charges out into the front yard, trips and falls down before raising her arms up to the heavens and shouting, *"Pearl!"*

These people are over the top, Shell thinks. Maybe he should just go home. He could just go back to the office and tell The Rotting Man he wants out of it. That way he wouldn't have to admit defeat. He could just make it sound like it was something he didn't want to do anymore. Might as well press on for the time being. It isn't like he has a lot of alternatives.

7

He walks away from the tree cutter and takes a blow to the back of the head. The pain is staggering, shooting through his entire body. Everything swims in front of him before going a washed-out kind of gray. His legs feel rubbery. In a city like this, in the midst of the slag plague, the last thing you want to give up is your vigilance but, unwillingly, he surrenders to unconsciousness and collapses to the ground.

He opens his eyes in a bright room. Surprisingly cool. He doesn't feel totally awake yet. A rancid smell surrounds him. He stares up at the water-stained ceiling and hears a male voice say: "He's clean. I checked him."

There's something comforting in that. By "clean," Shell assumes he means clean of slags. He has always dreaded the loss of consciousness, imagining he will wake up and find himself infested with slags, infected with the plague. The only place he really feels comfortable sleeping in is his room at home. It's in a city that has reasonably contained the slag infestation and his bedroom is guarded against that very thing—treated and secure. He wonders where he is. Maybe he's in the hospital. Maybe someone took advantage of the chaos to rob him when it was clear most people had other things on their minds. Maybe someone just attacked him because he was new and different. It certainly wouldn't have been the first time. As much as he tries not to seem like a detective, most people still figure him out. And most people confuse a detective with some type of authority figure even though that couldn't be further from the truth. He is not out to find and punish any evildoers. He only looks for people. And he will do whatever is necessary to find those people because it pays reasonably well. This often means breaking the law himself. He is more of a criminal than most of the people who confuse him for a cop. He doesn't like to think of himself as a bounty hunter. People get lost. People need finding. He is not the one who decides their ultimate fate.

"What'll we do with him?" A woman's voice. Shrill and old.

Shell turns his head to the right and surveys the room. It's completely wrecked. Large bookcases line the walls but all the books have been removed from the cases, strewn about the room, their pages ripped out. Furniture is overturned. Even the wallpaper hangs, ripped and shredded, from the walls. These must be more Pearl hunters. An old woman, presumably the one heard just a few moments ago, attempts to pull up the carpet. Her hair, sculpted into a tightly bound white perm, is unwavering. She wears a black bondage suit from the neck down, rendering her undoubtedly hideous body into a somewhat pleasing form.

"I guess we wake him up," the man's voice says.

Shell turns toward the voice. "I'm awake," he says, spotting the man.

Shell pulls himself up into a sitting position on the couch. The man, portly and older, dressed for leisure, uprights an orange chair and sits down in it, facing Shell. The man has a white beard and wears what seems to be a permanent smile, his head thrown back on his shoulders, his eyes little more than slits. He has a nasty cut on his forehead.

"Care for a smoke?" the man asks.

"Where am I?" Shell asks, adjusting his eyepatch and smoothing his meager amount of hair.

"I'm sorry," the old man says. "My name's Dave Happalance and this is my wife, Ingrid. You're in our home."

Shell makes to get up. "I really appreciate your hospitality and I'd really love to stay and chat but I have some business to tend to."

The man gestures for Shell to sit back down. A friendly gesture. Shell continues to stand. The man, Dave, with surprising agility, rises from his chair and pushes Shell back onto the couch. He smiles ridiculously the entire time.

"Ingrid. My pipe." The man continues to stare at Shell. Actually, with his eyes such slits, it's more like he just points his head at Shell. "I think you would find it beneficial to stay for a few minutes."

"Do I have a choice?" Shell says. "If I stand up you'll probably just push me back down."

"Probably," Dave says.

Ingrid brings Dave a pipe and a bag of something.

"You ever smoke these?" Dave asks, gesturing at the clear bag.

"I'm not sure what that is," Shell says.

Dave packs his pipe and hands the bag over to Shell.

Shell eyes the bag suspiciously. "Are those slags?"

"Indeed," Dave says. "They make a surprisingly good smoke." He flicks a match and touches it to the bowl of his pipe. Shell immediately identifies the source of the stink.

"Isn't that . . . bad for you?"

"Once dead there really isn't a lot of harm they can bring you. I used to have these imported from other cities but now they're all around. All I have to do is hop right out in the backyard and snag a jarful, put them in the oven for a few hours until they're all brown and toasty and . . . *voila!* Slagweed! Sure you don't want some?"

Dave holds the pipe out to him.

"I couldn't," Shell says. "I've been a little sick."

"I hear that's going around."

"Is that why you checked me?"

"Checked you?"

"Yeah, as I was waking up, I heard someone say, 'He's all clean.'"

Dave holds the pipe out to Ingrid, who takes a long pull.

"Oh, we weren't checking you for slags. We were checking to make sure you weren't hiding Pearl."

"How could I be hiding an eight-year-old child?"

Ingrid took another pull from the pipe, bracing herself on Dave's chair.

"She's not eight. She's the Queen of Town! How could she be eight?"

"It's just something I heard."

"No. She's always been around. However, she is very very small."

"Diminutive," Ingrid says, bending down and licking Dave on the cheek.

"Diminutive?" Shell says.

Dave holds his thumb and middle finger about six inches apart.

"That small?" Shell says, amazed. "It's hard to believe she's lasted this long."

"Well, she has all kinds of powers. She's not like normal people. Not at all like you or me."

"Of course not."

"By the way," Dave says. "I'd like to apologize for clubbing you in the head back there. I guess I just got so overwrought with the reward that momentarily, at least, I would have done anything for it. You have to understand my logic. Pearl goes missing. A stranger shows up. I thought maybe you had something to do with it."

Shell wants to react strongly to the man who clubbed him in the head but knows that if he gives this man the merciless beating he deserves he won't be able to get any information from him.

"So, do either of you have any ideas where she might be?"

Dave takes a large pull from the pipe, a fresh stink blossoms in the room and his face lights up. "Oh, sure, but I wouldn't tell you. Not with the reward out there. See, I don't really care whether or not Pearl is found. I think the city was probably better off before her."

"I thought you said she'd always been the Queen."

"I think I said she'd always been here. I don't think I said she'd always been Queen. Shit, I'm so high I don't know what I'm saying."

"So who was the Queen before Pearl?"

"I think I said she's always been the Queen."

"How can she have always been the Queen if she's only eight?"

"I *never* said she was only eight. She's very old. Ancient, even. But she's never grown up. She'll always be eight. And a very *small* eight, at that."

"What does the Queen of a mid-size city do?"

"If you ask me, she doesn't—*didn't*—do a whole lot."

"No?"

"No. The whole position was trumped up and overrated. Maybe she realized how useless she really was and decided to move on."

"Wouldn't that be strange for someone who has always been here?"

"There are so many things you're not aware of. Sometimes we all have to go out and find ourselves. You ever get lost? You ever feel like your *soul* got lost? If you ask me, that's the real plague. No one knows who they are anymore. How did you lose your eye?"

"How do you know I'm not just wearing this as some sort of crazy disguise?"

"I checked. It's grisly."

"I don't talk about it."

"You're bringing me down."

"Me too," Ingrid echoes before taking another massive pull from the pipe. She woozily leans over and begins licking Dave on the neck. He giggles. The cut on his forehead cracks open and unleashes a narrow trickle of blood.

"Actually," he says. "I was going to ask if *you* had any ideas where she might be . . ." His giggles become louder. More uncontrolled.

"I'm just a stranger passing through town," Shell says. "And I'm sorry but I really have to be going now."

The Happalances are lost to whatever sick game they're playing. Shell shakily stands up and exits through the front door, pausing only to vomit on their porch.

8

He looks up to see a luminescent child on a dirt bike pointing a Glock at him. Shell throws up his arms, like that's going to stop anything, just as the kid fires. It's completely dark out now and the shot is a fireball erupting from the gun. It all happens too fast for Shell to even dive out of the way. He hears a screech to his right and looks down. Half a mature slag wriggles in Shell's puke. His first thought is that he hopes the slag didn't come from him. His second thought is that maybe Hollow City has had a slag problem longer than they care to admit. Mature slags are rare. The size of an adult male forearm with teeth. If bitten by a mature slag, the victim has fewer than three hours to live.

The slightly glowing kid on the dirt bike has quite possibly saved his life.

"Come on, patchy. Hop on. I ain't got all night."

Shell hurries for the dirt bike. The kid looks like a gang member. Red bandana around his head. Sleeveless denim jacket over an equally sleeveless heavy metal t-shirt. Stonewashed jeans. Puffy gym shoes worn untied.

Shell hops on the dirt bike and looks back at the Happalances. Dave, now shirtless, rushes onto the porch and encloses his meaty hands around the slag. He licks his lips. There's a crazed look in his eyes, now open and round and huge. Behind him, Ingrid smacks his back with a riding crop.

Shell turns back to the kid on the bike. "Where are we going?"

"The store, fuckmunch. I gotta get some supplies. And booze. It's not a good night to be out. Can you handle a weapon?"

"Sure," Shell says.

The kid hands the Glock back to him. Shell holds it in his right hand. He's always been rather fond of the Glock, its angular Austrian lethality. It was designed to stop people. The owner of a Glock is not fucking around.

The kid pops the clutch and they speed down Main Street, zooming past a SWAT team unloading from a truck.

"Everything's coming to an end, douche," the kid says.

"What do you mean?"

"Hollow City. It's falling."

"That sounds pretty outdated. I don't even think that can happen anymore."

"What do you know, gramps?"

"Do you think you could stop calling me names?"

"I have to. It's what I'm all about. I don't kiss no one's ass. 'Sides, I could just throw you off my fuckin' bike."

"I'm not asking you to kiss my ass. I just think the name calling is uncalled for."

"Clever, asswipe."

"I am holding the gun."

"Don't you fuckin' threaten me!" the kid shouts. A mist of spittle covers Shell's face. "I'll fuckin' slit your throat and leave you in a goddamn ditch! You don't know what's goin' on."

"Maybe you could tell me."

"I'm not tellin' you shit."

"Fine."

They ride for a while, the only sound the high-pitched whine of the dirt bike. They leave the city proper and enter a series of back roads, corn and soybeans growing all around them.

Shell works with what he has. He is here to find Pearl. She is, or used to be, the Queen of Town. She's small. She might be eight. She might be ancient. She might be ancient but mildly retarded. Everyone is looking for her either because they love her as their queen or because there is a sizable reward for finding her. Allegedly, the last person to see her was someone named Mike. Why would The Rotting Man send him to find her? And when he finds her, he's supposed to take her back to The Rotting Man. Or is he? The Rotting Man never really said. He's usually more specific about these things. He'll have to call The Rotting Man if he finds her. The prospects of Shell's finding her, he thinks, are amazingly small. He only finds about half the people he searches for and, most of the time, it's not like this. This feels like a race. With everyone looking for her, he'll have to be the *first* to find her. And he doesn't know this town nearly as well as people who have lived here their entire lives. Which could be to his advantage . . .

The dirt bike plows into a pothole and Shell's concentration shatters as it wobbles violently back and forth. The boy expertly straightens out and they are once again cruising smoothly along.

"What's your name?" Shell asks.

"Used to be Mike but I changed it to Kid Rider."

Shell suppresses a laugh. That's an awful name. But his previous name . . . that could be something.

"Why the change?"

"I escaped from the House of Mikes. And don't fuckin' condensate to me."

"The House of Mikes?" This is the most promising thing Shell has heard all evening. It even takes his mind off Kid Rider's atrocious use of words.

"That's what I said, buttmunch. See, Hollow City had too many Mikes so they put 'em all in a house on the outside of town. They was all given a number and a chance to live around themselves. It was supposed to help us establish an identity but it was terrible. The lower numbers pulled rank because they were there first. I was Mike 31. A hardluck fuckin' number. Thirteen backwards. Like ass rape. I'll show you the tattoo when we get to the store. I definitely didn't get no breaks. That place was a fuckin' prison."

"Did you know Pearl?"

"Shit no, man. She wouldn't have nothin' to do with me, dicklips. She started hangin' around the House but she was only interested in the lower numbers like maybe 1 through 4. Why? You lookin' for her too?"

"Are you?"

"In my own way, I guess."

"Why are you looking for her?"

"Without her, Hollow City ain't for shit. Without her, people just run around doin' whatever they wanna do and then it gets to be just like the House. And it ain't just the people either. You see that slag I capped back there? That wouldn'ta been around if the Queen was here . . ."

"Why not?"

"I don't know, man. You ask too many questions. She had like powers or something." Happalance had mentioned something to that effect, as well. Shell adds it to his mental list. Magical powers.

"You talk about her like she's dead."

"Well she ain't *here*, is she? Best to assume the worst."

They are on a narrow country road. A corona of light floats in the distance. "Is that the store?"

"Sure is."

"Do you drive this thing when you're all boozed up?"

"Totally fuckin' crocked, man!" Kid Rider laughs. Shell spares him the lecture.

"You know what you remind me of, man?"

"A walking asshole?" Shell guesses.

"No! A fuckin' pirate! With that eyepatch and shit!"

"Gee. I've never heard that one before."

"Arrgh. Shiver me timbers, matey!"

For laughs, Shell places the tip of the gun against the back of Kid Rider's head.

"Knock it off," Shell says.

"Okay. Okay. I was just kiddin'. You shouldn't aim a gun at someone unless you plan on usin' it."

"You want me to?"

"Fuck off, Long John."

Kid Rider veers sharply to the right and into the parking lot of the store. A lonely gas pump adorns the deserted parking lot.

9

They dismount the bike and walk into the bright fluorescence of the store, Shell tucking the gun into the back of his pants. Even in this day of the slags, it's not a good idea to walk into a store with a drawn weapon. It doesn't seem to have any kind of name. Kid Rider comes up to Shell's nipples. He holds his arms away from his body and puffs up his chest like he's well-muscled, vigilantly turning his head from side to side. He heads to the back, to the booze, and Shell decides to question the young black-haired cashier. She wears a lot of makeup and looks kind of skanky. Her shirt is black and says, in bright pink letters: SUMMA THIS. It is stretched tightly across her small breasts.

"Hi," she says.

"Hi. Do you know how I could get to the House of Mikes?"

"Why?" She chuckles. "Your name Mike?"

"No. But all my friends are named Mike."

"You just continue on out this road here until you see a big house. I mean really big. That's it. They have to fit a lot of Mikes in there. If you reach Fugueland you've gone too far."

"Fugueland?"

"Don't ask."

"I see. Do you sell the paper?"

She gestures to a small wire container below the front of the counter. "Only a couple left."

Shell picks one up. It's about six pages covered in crayon drawings and letters and stapled on the left-hand side. It looks like it was done by a child. The letters are all very large and crooked. Most of the words are misspelled. Shell doesn't imagine it'll be very informative and places it back in the container. The cashier snaps her gum and waits for Kid Rider to bring his fifth of whiskey and bucket of slag repellant to the counter.

"Who's paying?" the cashier asks.

"He is," Kid Rider gestures toward Shell. "I'm not nearly old enough to buy whiskey."

"Okay. Get back here," the cashier says.

"Excuse me?" Shell asks.

"Come on. You have to fuck me. That's the payment."

"That's the payment," Kid Rider echoes. "I'll leave you two alone." He exits the store. Shell watches him to make sure he doesn't drive off.

"Come on. It'll be quick," she says.

"I'm not even hard," Shell says. "And I don't feel very well."

"Just get back here."

Shell walks around the counter until he's standing behind it. He's never been behind the counter of a convenience store before. He finds it kind of exciting. The girl wears a short black skirt, fishnet stockings and combat boots, which he also finds kind of exciting. She leans against the counter, her back to him, and lifts her skirt up over red underwear. She slides those down and rubs her ass.

"I'll need a condom," Shell says, suddenly hard.

"There's plenty right back there." She throws a hand over her shoulder.

He opens the box, takes the gun from the back of his pants, places it on the counter behind him, unbuttons and unzips his pants, slides them down, tears the condom from its foil wrapper and un-rolls it onto his cock, the sterile smell of latex and spermicide hitting his nostrils. He probes her sex with a finger, making sure she's wet. She is.

"I'm always wet," she says.

"Um . . . good?" Shell says.

"Better for everyone."

He slides into her slowly and comes almost immediately. It feels like the walls of her vagina are quivering, pulsing around his spurting penis.

"Told you it wouldn't take long."

He pulls out and hears a sickeningly familiar plop. Three slags are writhing on the floor between the cashier's boots.

"Oh God," he says. He loses it. Vomits on the back of the cashier.

"What the fuck?!" she says. She reaches down and pulls a slag from her inner thigh. "Oh shit," she says, vomiting onto the floor.

"I gotta go." Shell hitches up his pants, grabs the gun, and heads out into the parking lot.

Kid Rider stands in front of the open bucket of repellant, covering himself in the powder. This, apparently, is what makes him luminescent.

"Want some before I close it up?" he asks.

"Why not," Shell says, still shaken. He covers himself with the glowing powder, dropping a little down his pants for good measure.

Then he faces Kid Rider and says, "You're not gonna like this."

"What?" Kid Rider is slightly shocked, expecting the worst.

Shell levels the gun at him. "I'm taking this." He holds the gun up. "And I'm taking the bike."

"You fuckin' cranksucker. I saved your fuckin' life."

"I know. And I do apologize. I just can't be held responsible for a minor. If I ever see you again, I'll give it all back."

10

He slams the Glock down the back of his pants and mounts the bike. He wants to look cool driving away but he's almost too large to control it and tips it over, skidding across the parking lot. He hears Kid Rider running for it and pulls the gun back out. "Stay away!" he shouts. "I'm okay." Kid Rider freezes. Shell puts the gun back, uprights the bike, mounts it and speeds away into the night. Smoother this time.

He isn't on the road for long until he reaches what has to be the House of Mikes. He checks his watch. It's nearly two o'clock in the morning. The whole night has been a blur and he doesn't think he's any closer to finding Pearl than when he first started. Behind the House of Mikes are a couple banks of floodlights. Shell dismounts and hears cheering and shouting coming from back there. He wonders if he should pull the gun out and keep it in his hand. Are the Mikes dangerous? Well, if they are, he figures it's probably best not to put them immediately on guard.

He walks around the large house and sees a circle of people gathered around something. A few of the Mikes are walking from the house, probably to watch whatever spectacle is being played out. They all seem to be slightly different, which means they are also slightly the same. Short hair. A little meat on their bones. All shirtless and wearing khaki trousers. Each of them has a large number tattooed on his chest. Shell guesses the number is permanent. Once a 25, always a 25. So says the tattoo.

He imagines, perhaps from what Kid Rider said, the Mikes to be a closed society but he is welcomed immediately.

"Hey!" Mike 16 shouts. "You gotta come and watch this! We're practicing Mike control."

Shell wanders over to the circle of men. They surround a pit. In the pit is a boy with the number 38 on his torso. Also in the pit are three mature slags. They snap at the boy as he frantically tries to climb the dirt wall. Shell doesn't want to watch this but, at the same time, he needs to find a Mike who can supply him with information about Pearl. Most likely Mikes 1 through 4.

Watching the boy try to get away from the slags, Shell has a revelation.

He no longer cares about finding Pearl. What is one girl's life, even if she is a queen, in exchange for someone else's? There are enough people looking for Pearl. There is a sizable reward for finding her. But what about this boy who is trying so desperately to get away from the slags? Born into Mikedom. Handed over by his Mike brothers, turned into some form of perverse entertainment.

Of course, he never really cared about finding Pearl in the first place. He cared about the money. He still cares about the money but fears he may have to end up writing it off.

Nevertheless, he can't stand around and watch this kid get devoured by slags.

Shell pulls the Glock out and fires down into the pit.

The Mike in the pit drops to his knees and covers his ears as the first slag explodes. Shell aims again and fires. The second slag explodes. The third slag, now desperate and alone, makes a lunge for the boy. Shell fires again and catches it in mid-flight, its toothy head disintegrating.

"Aw, man," Mike 12 says. "We was just havin' fun."

"That is not the way to have fun," Shell says.

"Who the fuck are you? Your name ain't Mike," Mike 6 says.

Shell holds the gun out in front of him, suddenly feeling very threatened.

"I need to speak with Mike 1, 2, 3 or 4. And one of you needs to help that kid out of the hole."

"Well, Mike 2's dead," Mike 18 says. "He's been dead for years. As for the other Mikes, they're fulfilling their civic duty by searching for the Queen."

"What can you tell me about the Queen? I heard she used to come here a lot."

"I wouldn't say a lot."

"But you've met her?"

"Sure, I've met her."

"Have any ideas where she might be?"

"If I had any ideas where she might be then I'd be the one out there looking for her instead of the other Mikes."

"Do you know anyone who would want to kidnap her or hurt her?"

"No, man, everybody loved the Queen."

"Is this true?" he asks the rest of the Mikes.

They all nod their melon-sized heads.

"What wasn't to like? She was just a little old lady who didn't have any real power anyway."

"A little old lady?"

"Shit. I don't know. I always thought she was old. I never got too close to her. All I know is she's real small. Most queens are old, I thought."

"How do you feel now that she's gone?"

"Well, I feel like hell. She was the life of this city. I don't know how to explain it exactly. It was just . . . just good to have her around, you know?"

"What will I find if I go to Fugueland?"

"You don't want to go there."

"Why not?"

"Nobody goes there. It's dangerous."

"Dangerous how?"

"It's why they call this place Hollow City. Fugueland empties people out. I don't know how it does but . . . people who go there, they ain't the same when they come back. But, like I said, no one goes there anymore."

"Thanks," Shell says, turning to leave. "You've all been a big help."

"Mister?" Mike 18 says. "You ain't goin' there, are ya?"

"I think I have to," Shell says, turning his back on the Mikes and heading for his bike.

INTERLUDE: FUGUELAND

BIRTH

The bike long discarded he comes upon Fugueland. No. There are no blinding lights. No carnival signs. Just a swirling mass like a fogbank and standing there looking at it he feels life catch up with him. His body aches. His empty socket throbs beneath the patch. Nausea continues to gnaw at his stomach and head. Shell. He finally feels like his name. Takes a deep breath. Puts the gun down. Sheds his clothes and steps into something very much like pure consciousness. Each droplet clings to his skin and he feels it and he likes the way it feels and even though his eye is open it might as well be closed because he can't see anything. The gray darkens but he doesn't see it. He feels it. Darkens all the way to black. Deep space black. And he's floating through this space and is suddenly aware it is not space at all but the womb and the womb smells like the earth. All the dark rich fertile loam of things long dead and things coming back to life and when he reaches out he clasps two handfuls of dirt and pulls away at them. Rending the womb. Opening the womb to the outside world and he pours out screaming.

LIFE

And comes to a plateau of sorts. Flat smooth earth and he's at the top of something maybe the top of everything and this is all new to him and this feeling of newness feels good. He's all emptied out and this lack of insides makes him less aware of his outsides. But awareness builds. He feels his bones coming up from nothing. Massing around themselves. And he feels his muscles and his nerves take shape and strengthen and then his skin. Blood chugs through everything and he takes his first deep breaths and fills his lungs with this unsullied air. Aware of his solidity in this space. He approaches the edge of the plateau and looks out onto a world not yet built. He knows what is to come. It hits him in a single blinding flash of knowledge. The people will come. The buildings will come. The cultures will come and with them will come all those dangerous human emotions. With them will come everything that can gnaw a person away from the inside. And he is also aware of the inescapability of that. He becomes aware of life's grim march. Onward. Forever onward. Meeting whatever cruel fate awaits but it is through this cruel fate and face of humanity that true beauty can shine. No death is a good death but all death is inevitable. He turns to meet it. Casting out his insides to the blank world around. Hollow. Full. And now hollow again. Approaching through the fog is a pack of wolves. Except for their heads. Their heads are the tapered tooth-rimmed heads of mature slags. He lies down on the cool earth. Feels the air swirl around him and drop down onto his face and kiss his lips as the first of the slag wolves bites into his flesh.

A KIND OF DEATH

It's a mangled form emerging from Fugueland. Whole on the outside. Slagwolf-gnawed on the inside. The human body is an ever-expanding collection of things some of which have to be trimmed away. Sometimes death is necessary. It gives us something to bury far beneath the ground so more light can shine on the life that is left. Some people are here. Some people have always been here. Some people deserve to live. Some people deserve to die. He is only the messenger. Only the envelope. Only the shell. He could break and crumble at any minute.

11

Shell dons his clothes, mounts the dirt bike, and heads back into town. He isn't sure what just happened to him. The taste of vomit lingers on his tongue but he feels a renewed sense of purpose. He will look for Pearl in one last place and, if she isn't there, he's decided to go back home and quit the agency. And if he decides he can't live without the agency, can't live without a job, then he'll take a gun and put it in his mouth or perhaps his hollow eye and pull the trigger. Maybe the Mikes were right about Fugueland but Shell doesn't know if being a different person is a good thing or a bad thing. The world certainly doesn't need *more* people like him.

The final shreds of darkness are still all around him and he can feel the immense weight of the day breathing a sunny whisper on the other side of the curtains.

It's dawn by the time he gets back to the apartment. He's tried to shut everything else out of his mind and concentrate only on finding Pearl. Everything else will have to wait. Fuck everything else. Whether he finds her or not, he's decided this is his last hurrah. He might as well go out with a bang.

He thinks about Mr. Happalance saying Pearl has always been here. He thinks about Mr. Blatz saying Miss Fitch has always been here. He thinks about the man in overalls saying everyone was looking for Pearl. Shell knows someone who is not looking for Pearl. He knows someone so wrapped up in psychotic insanity she has to drag herself from the living room. Hollow City. Okay. So some people are hollow. Some people make good vessels. Maybe Pearl is in the apartment. Maybe Pearl is in Miss Fitch. Maybe her psychosis is the act of a diminutive Queen trying to fight her way out. Maybe Pearl has chosen to hide in the one place where she will go undetected. The insides of every other house are devastated, torn apart by people, the occupants, searching for Pearl.

Shell figures it's time to do some devastation of his own.

He pulls up in front of the building. Main Street at dawn is only slightly buzzing. Trash and the insides of people's homes, often one in the same, line the street. The sound of the chainsaw continues to rip through the air. He makes sure the Glock is still tucked into the back of his pants.

He opens the door to his building and crosses the kitchen. Miss Fitch lies face down in the living room. She is covered in slags. Shell kicks some from her hand, grabs it, and drags her into the kitchen. He then goes about ripping the building apart. Cabinet doors torn from hinges and then the cabinets themselves from the walls. Cushions and beds ripped apart. Carpet up. Drywall smashed. Nothing. Nothing. And more nothing.

Panting, sweaty, and out of breath, Shell maneuvers into the kitchen and picks a butcher knife up from the covered floor. He rolls Miss Fitch over and doesn't even bother to feel for a pulse. Briefly, he feels a sense of contradiction. How could he save that kid at the Mikes at the possible expense of Pearl and then open up this woman to find her? The feeling passes. He wills it to. If Miss Fitch isn't dead yet with all those slags writhing on her, she will be soon. Miss Fitch isn't doing anyone any good. The people of Hollow City *need* Pearl,

Shell convinces himself. Because convincing himself of that is better than believing he wants the money or wants to go out on a memorable note. It seems too perfect. The only thing that could make it more perfect would be if Miss Fitch were named Miss Oyster. Open the oyster, find the Pearl.

Shell slashes her from the hollow of her throat down through her rotten sex. Gullet to groin.

And there's nothing inside. She's filled with slags. Absolutely packed with them. Shell hopes his repellant is still active. He stands, takes a deep breath, and lets the knife drop to the floor. He wanders outside to vomit and just keeps wandering home.

13

The Rotting Man sits behind his desk, plump, gray, and stinking. A small pile of cash sits on the left-hand side of the desk. His once white dress shirt is stained yellow at the shoulders and plastered to his skin. Shell sits facing him.

"I failed," he says.

"You gave it your best. We can't all be winners."

Cliché after cliché after cliché.

Even though he spouts words of encouragement, The Rotting Man looks unusually depressed. He pushes his glasses up his fleshy nose with his right hand, turned a purplish gray with the rot. "I am sorry to say, however, that you will not be receiving any of this." He pushes the pile of cash off the desk with his left hand. It hits the floor and scatters only slightly in a puddle of fetid fluid.

"I think I'm giving it up anyway," Shell says.

"Quitting the agency?"

"Yep."

"But you're the best detective we have . . . In fact, you're the only detective we have . . ."

"And a failure."

"Come on now. You're too hard on yourself. Tell me: when you were out there in Hollow City . . . they ever tell you how *small* Pearl was?"

"Pretty small. Diminutive."

"That's a pretty fancy word. You pick that up there?"

"Yeah. Well, I kind of knew what it meant. That was probably the first time I'd ever heard it in conversation. This was an interesting case. I know you have confidentiality clauses with your clients but, seeing as this is my last one, I was wondering if you could tell me who was offering to pay you for looking for Pearl and what exactly they wanted with her."

The Rotting Man looks down at his desk and shakes his head. "You're right," he says. "This was a strange case because there was no client. Actually, I guess there was. The client was Hollow City. It was an open reward. To the first person who finds her."

"I knew that."

"I was going to give you this amount," he gestures to the sopping money on the floor. "And take Pearl back to Hollow City, claiming to have found her myself. Their reward was roughly double what I offered you."

"Actually, you didn't offer me anything. I just assumed it was the standard amount."

"Which it was."

"Which is probably why you never went into specifics."

"Could be. I needed someone who could bring her back here without anyone ever knowing it. Or else they would have pounced on you, restored Pearl, and given the reward to you."

"You really are a greedy shit."

"I know. That's what this business is all about. Pure greed. Anyway, it'll be tough to see you go."

"It's not just the failing. I haven't been feeling well lately. Nauseous all the time . . ."

"Maybe you have a parasite or something."

The Rotting Man holds his middle finger and thumb about six inches apart. Shell notices he has lost a pinky since the last time they met in person. "They say she was about that big? Say anything about her 'magical powers'?"

Shell nods.

"Maybe more like this?" The Rotting Man decreases the size considerably. "Do me a favor before you go—just to satisfy my morbid curiosity—let me see what's under the eyepatch. You never have told me how you lost it."

"My ex-wife plucked it out during our last great battle. It's kind of gross-looking."

Shell slides his chair back from the desk and stands up.

"You visit Fugueland while you were there?" The Rotting Man asks.

"I don't know what you're talking about." Shell leans over the desk. He's kind of nervous. He's never voluntarily shown anyone what was under the patch before.

"That's where I caught the rot," The Rotting Man says, standing up to meet Shell over the desk. "Yep. Many years ago. I used to live there. In Hollow City."

"I never knew that." Shell puts his fingers on the patch and lifts it up, seeing his reflection in The Rotting Man's glasses.

He sees The Rotting Man tense up and, in the reflection, he sees why.

A brown eye stares back at him. He moves his fingers up to poke at it. How did that get there?

"You have her," The Rotting Man says. "That's her eye."

Shell takes a step back.

The Rotting Man unleashes a noxious stink.

"So what if I do?" Shell asks.

"She's mine."

"Actually, she's the people of Hollow City's. If anyone's."

"She's in you. I need her powers. They're the only thing that can stop the rot."

"And now we come to the truth. I think I'll take her back myself. Maybe I'll take the reward."

"You won't." The Rotting Man throws open a drawer and removes a huge, antique revolver. Shell immediately regrets leaving the Glock at home.

"If you shoot me then she'll die too."

"I only need a little bit of her power. And then you'll be free. Both of you will be free."

Suddenly, Shell feels a whole other system of thoughts move in his brain. It takes control of his brain, his processes, and he feels himself recede to the back of his skull.

"I've never been free," the Queen says loudly, with Shell's voice, with Shell's mouth. "So you want to keep me here as a cure for your sick condition or take me back and throw me to a pack of sycophants. I don't see how I can win."

The Rotting Man thumbs a button under his desk. The lock in his door clicks closed.

"Heal me," The Rotting Man says through rotting lips.

"Let me go," the Queen says.

"Just touch me in the rotting parts. Please."

Pearl moves Shell's arm across the desk, within an inch of The Rotting Man's torso, hovering just in front of it, before driving the fist forward, into the feverish insides of The Rotting Man's body. The Rotting Man chokes on his insides, aims his gun, and fires for Shell's heart but hits his shoulder instead. Shell is thrown back into the door and, looking at The Rotting Man standing there with the gun in his hand, doomed but bent on destruction anyway, he feels a giant force build inside. It starts at the base of his spine, works its way up through the back of his throat and erupts from his mouth.

The Rotting Man is driven against the back wall by this invisible force. He continues to gargle and spew and now he is rotting at an alarming rate, the stench of putrefaction filling the room as his insides explode from puffy, rotted flesh to land on the dingy tiled floor. The gun falls to the ground and it isn't long before The Rotting Man is a pile of dried meat and bones.

The Queen directs Shell's body outside into the gray summer afternoon.

14

An unlikely pair, Pearl and Shell drift as one into a dim, narrow alley. The conscienceless Shell and the consciousness of a whole town. Shell's insides feel swollen. He drops to his knees, bracing himself against the grimy brick wall. He feels his skin stretch to bursting and then further. Ripping. He can hear it rip and he wants to scream, wants to cry out but doesn't want to attract attention and, besides, Pearl controls his mouth. And she, apparently, doesn't feel like screaming at all.

Shell collapses onto his back and watches Pearl rise from his split flesh. She is not diminutive in the least. She is a beautiful young woman who looks lovingly down at him. She places her index finger over her lips, "Shhh," and reaches down toward Shell. She takes a fragment of bone from his rib and a long strand of her hair. The bone becomes a needle and she feeds the hair through its eye.

Within a few minutes he is all stitched up but strangely flat. She leans toward him and at first he thinks she's going to kiss him. Instead, she lifts up his eyepatch, encloses her generous lips around the socket and exhales. Shell watches his body inflate and feels her breath move through his insides. He coughs, dragging himself up into a sitting position. He doesn't feel so sick anymore. In fact, he feels kind of great.

"Why?" he asks. "Why all this?"

"To get away," her actual voice is soft yet authoritative.

"Away from what?"

"Hollow City. I don't know. Everyone."

"Being adored must be difficult."

"It is if that's not what you want. Or maybe it's because it's the only thing you've ever known."

"So you get to just walk away?"

"It looks like it. But think about it. You get to be a human again."

"I've always been a human."

"You call what you used to do for a living being human?"

Shell shrugs and says, "It put food on the table," and feels like The Rotting Man.

"I guess you'll justify it however you see fit."

"Since you're so pious, how do you justify leaving your city in ruins?"

"I'm sure I'll be back to pick up the pieces. Eventually. They need a little self-sufficiency. Besides, it's not really in ruins. They're just crazy because they've always had me to look after them. Maybe they'll grow up."

"Speaking of growing up—I thought you were, you know, diminutive."

"I was. Now I'm not."

"It was Happalance, wasn't it?"

"I shall not tell."

"Yeah, Happalance put you in my eye socket and . . ."

"You can sit here speculating all you want to but I've gotta go. There's a whole world out there to see."

She walks down the alley, toward the city street, and Shell feels a brief pang of regret. Regret and pity. He fears for her insides and wonders how long it will take them to become devastated and smashed. He hopes they won't. He hopes the world she wants to see is still here a little longer. He stands up, coughs, adjusts his eyepatch and heads home. He has to find a new job.

PART TWO

VINCENT SEVERITY

Months earlier...

1

Amber Toulouse gags a little when she turns on the light in the break room. She was going to grab her half-eaten sandwich from the refrigerator but decides to leave it. The break room smells like decay and looks like some kind of maggot infestation has taken hold over in the corner near the trash can. She turns off the light and shuts the door. Let the cleaning crew deal with it. Maggots are not in her job description. She decides she can probably just call it quits and go home.

She works in the office of Ames Construction. Times are slow. Nobody seems to be building anything. She's taken like three calls all day and the other lady in the office, Martha Sleeveless, went home around noon. Said she was feeling sick. Amber thought it was more like she was feeling bored and it was a gorgeous Friday and the construction crew hadn't come in at all today.

She turns off all the lights in the office and heads to her desk to turn off the computer and radio and grab her purse. As she puts her hand on the radio's switch, she pauses at the word "quarantine." She listens for a couple more seconds.

"The Mayor also advised all residents of Scruffington, New York, to stay within the town's perimeters. It is also advised that travelers bypass the city."

Hysteria, she thinks, and flips the switch. Just some burg in New York. By Monday, the Mayor will be rolling out a travel brochure for Scruffington. Quarantine would kill the economy. Besides, that is New York. This is Ohio. She doesn't really care what happens in New York.

"Joey Ramone!" she shouts and shakes it away, slinging her giant canvas purse over her shoulder and heading for the door. The office really does smell rank. She wonders if she should call the owner and then decides she doesn't want to talk to him. She pulls the door shut and locks it, heading down the hallway and the stairs until she is out in the bright sunlight.

2

Some people look straight ahead when they walk. Some people, dreamers mostly, look up at the sky. They are usually clumsy, always running into things. Amber is a head down kind of walker. A psychiatrist would probably say this is because of low self-esteem.

"Elvis Costello!"

She listens to her voice blare out in the early summer light thinking it doesn't really sound much like her voice at all. The only time she ever shouts is when she has to shout the names. She turns to head into the alley she claimed as her shortcut after starting this job nearly a year ago. She can't wait to get home and change out of her dress shoes and skirt, dump her giant purse. And her shirt has felt more binding as the day progressed.

She looks up and sees a tacky blue El Camino blocking the exit of the alley. Her heart jumps. Adrenaline not usually there becomes a torrent under her skin. Probably just someone doing a crazy ass parking job. She has never had any problems with the alley before. Muttering curses, she turns to head back out to the sidewalk when a man grabs the back of her neck. She nearly shouts "Ian Curtis!" but is cut off. The man quickly and expertly covers her mouth in duct tape.

Immediately, she knows what is happening but it still has a dreamlike quality to it. She has to get away. She knows this much. She springs forward, not caring who the hell is gripping her arms in his powerful hands. But all her energy is useless. He slams her down on the asphalt, wrapping her wrists together with twirl after twirl of the tape. Then he picks her up and slings her over his shoulder.

Is he taking her to the car? That's where she thinks he's heading but the only thing she can see is the bottom of his jacket and his powerful-looking legs covered in tight blue jeans. He clutches her purse in the hand not restraining her. Maybe somebody will see her before he can get her into the car. These kinds of things did not happen in Celine. Of course, it is really too early in the afternoon for anyone to be out and about. School hasn't even let out yet and the lunch rush is over.

Keeping her on his shoulder by pressing his right hand down on her ass, the man pulls open the passenger side door with the hand holding the purse and throws her in. Rather than wasting time to circle the car and reach the driver's side, he crawls over her and slides deftly into the driver's seat, covering her with the smell of his heavy cologne. He stuffs her purse behind the seat. She quickly swings her legs up on the vinyl seat and kicks at the man. Kicks at his square head with the black plastic-looking hair and the tightly clipped black mustache that makes him look like a loose-cannon cop in a horrible seventies action show. But he smothers her legs and, for a brief and horrifying second, she thinks he is going to rape her right there in the car. Her skirt slides up her legs, virginal white underwear in plain view. He brings the tape up, snarls at her, and wraps it tightly around her ankles.

"Frank Zappa!" her brain screams. No. It is her brain commanding her mouth but her mouth won't move.

The man reaches across the seat and grabs her hard in between her collarbone and neck.

"Now you listen here, Amber." He speaks quickly, his voice sharp and clipped. "My name's Vincent and I do very severe things. I'm a very severe man. You don't wanna fuck with me. Now I'm just gonna take you someplace and we're gonna have us a little talk. And if you even think about screamin' for help or tryin' to get away you can kiss your ass goodbye. You can kiss your family's ass goodbye too. I'm a very severe man. I do very severe things." He continues to stare at her, that strange snarl fixed on his face. She looks into his eyes and doesn't quite know what it is she sees there. Madness, definitely, but something else.

He reaches into his shiny, tight brown leather jacket and pulls a very sharp-looking knife from its inside pocket. Holding the knife in his left hand, he reaches down with his right and squeezes her left nipple hard. She screams almost inaudibly and takes in a breath only to get a mouthful of the chemical-tasting tape.

"Nyah," he says, continuing to squeeze her nipple. "Your nipples ain't nothin'. Them's just tiny little bitty things. I'll show you what a nice big nipple looks like."

Finally releasing her, he reaches down to his belt and pulls his heavily starched shirt up to the top of his stomach. There, just to the right of his navel, is a nipple the size of a silver dollar.

"Now that there's a big nipple. Too bad its owner was a screamer. She screamed and screamed and didn't amount to shit. I'm a very severe man. I had to do it. I do very severe things."

Then another look, maybe reflection, creeps into his eerie brown eyes and he stares out the windshield for just a moment before saying, in a softer voice, "But that was before you. That was all before you, Amber Toulouse."

He pronounces her last name all wrong and she wonders who the hell he is. Turning the key in the ignition, he pulls away from the alley and drives out of Celine. Amber feels her hope sliding away. She wants to continue working against the heavy tape but she doesn't know what Vincent will do if she escapes. She likes her nipples where they are. As they drive along the state route, Amber blurts "Iggy Pop!" against the tape but Vincent shoots her a hateful stare, reaches out and whacks her on the skull, lightning-quick, with the haft of his knife.

He will never understand, she thinks. He will never understand how she *has* to shout the names. Does he know what will happen if she doesn't shout the names? A plague. A swirling plague will cover up the sun and form a black cloud and it will drop down on them, on everyone, and burn them all up with fever and disease. *That's* what will happen if she doesn't shout the names. She knows it.

3

Vincent continues powering the car, pushing the speed limit but never going more than five miles over it. He is a very severe man, Amber muses over what he said. He even looks severe. His tan skin shiny and taut over high cheekbones. His head sits on his shoulders without the visual benefit of a neck. She figures he probably isn't much taller than her but there is an aura of strength about him. Like a much larger man's power is compacted into his smaller frame.

As he drives, he continues to play with the nipple on his stomach. She wonders how he got it to stay on there. It does not become aroused as he strokes it with a fingertip. She can't watch anymore. How much longer does she have before that nipple becomes hers, unclothed and clenched between his severe fingers? She doesn't want to think about it. She turns her head to look out at the darkening countryside passing by the window and screams against the tape, "Jeff Buckley!"

4

They pull into another town that announces itself as being "MILTON—HOME OF THE UNIQUE LOZENGE" on a battered sign by the side of the road. The sunlight is dying, turning shadows to monsters. Vincent decides he wants to drive through the McDonald's and get some coffee. Amber wonders what a unique lozenge is.

"Now I'm gonna take the tape off your mouth," he says before they pull into the parking lot. "But so help me if you say one goddamn word or cry for help then I'm gonna take this car to the woods and fuck you so hard you'll be able to taste your pussy in the back of your throat. And I can do it before the police ever get there. Understand?"

She nods her head, not really knowing if she will cry for help or not. He reaches up and runs a rough hand down her sweaty cheek. It seems like she has been sweating constantly since he grabbed her out of the alley. He runs his fingers down to a jutting edge of the tape. The tape is not just over her mouth, it is wrapped around her head a couple of times. He grabs the tape and quickly unfurls it around her head, taking hair and skin along with it. She tries her best not to bark out in pain.

He points a short, stocky finger at her. "I mean it," he says. "Not one goddamn word or you won't be nothin' to me."

Again, she nods solemnly. She knows he's serious about his threats. His very severe threats.

He holds the knife up so she can see it and hides it between two buttons in the front of his shirt so she knows it's there, within his reach, if she decides to yell for help. He pulls through the drive-thru and barks into the speaker.

"I wanna big coffee!"

"One large coffee?"

"Yeah!"

The woman gives him the total and asks him to please pull around. He gets to the first window and pays, giving Amber a stern look of warning in between the first and second windows. At the second window, two things happen nearly simultaneously and

Amber feels like she is going to be murdered for sure. Wait, make that *raped* and murdered. Vincent was very clear about the rape.

The first thing that happens is that the worker woman must not have put the lid on the cup of coffee very tightly. She leans out to hand the cup to Vincent and he takes it quickly, severely, and the steaming hot coffee sloshes out into his crotch. At that exact moment, Amber shouts "Morrissey!" Vincent looks over at her, but she can tell he is seething about the coffee. The woman leans out the window and apologizes profusely. Vincent pinches his face up into a snarl, holding the coffee cup in his right hand before flinging its contents into the woman's face. Screaming, she immediately retreats back through the window.

Vincent wastes no time at all. He pounds the accelerator and the car (or is it a truck?) lurches into the street and they speed away through town. He laughs sarcastically, mockingly, beneath his breath and the back of his hand lashes across Amber's face. Her head snaps back and cracks into the window. He reaches down between her legs and grabs, shaking her crotch vigorously. His fingers dig against her perineum and the heel of his hand is heavy on her pubic mound.

"Mmmmm . . ." he snarls. "You got lucky back there, bitchy miss. If that nigger hadn't fucked with my coffee I would tear you apart right now. She deserved that though. She deserved all of it. Don't you think for a second she didn't. I'm a very severe man. She should have known I was a severe man. Then I woulda got the service I deserved."

He pulls his hand out of her sweaty crotch and pushes his fingertips beneath her nose.

"Smell that? That's the smell of a bitch in heat. All bitches are in heat. Look at you, squirmin' around in that seat just beggin' to be fucked. I bet you ain't never been fucked, have ya?"

He is wrong. She has had a boyfriend since she was seventeen and he has fucked her often since they started going out. But she doesn't think that is what Vincent wants to hear so she shakes her head.

"Well, bitchy Sue, you can talk now. Guess it don't make no fuckin' difference. I *told* you not to say a word! What was that shit you was shoutin'?"

"I couldn't help it."

"What do you mean you couldn't help it?"

"I have a condition."

"A condition?"

"Yeah."

"What kinda condition?"

"I guess it's like Tourette's. I have to shout the names of male vocalists."

"You mean like singers?"

"Yeah."

"How long you had that?"

"Ever since I can remember. Ever since I heard The Beatles for the first time."

"You're crazy," he pronounces as though this topic is not up for speculation. "Besides, The Beatles were a bunch of fags. I'm glad someone plugged John Lennon."

"Kurt Cobain!"

Vincent cringes visibly.

"Where are you taking me?"

"You should stop talking now."

Vincent bends toward the wheel, his head quickly ticking up to make sure the McDonald's incident hasn't resulted in someone calling the police on him. Soon they are on an ill-maintained country road and, the sun bloated and fat on the horizon, they pull up a long gravel driveway. There is a house up at the top. It's a small ranch house and Amber can tell, even from this distance, that it is not kept up very well. The neighboring houses are very far away.

Out of shouting distance, she thinks. Watching the huge ball of the sun, she feels very far from home.

5

Reaching the top of the driveway, Vincent pulls the car behind the house. Probably so no one would be able to see it from the road, Amber thinks. He kills the engine and gets out, walking purposefully around the front of the car and slinging the passenger side door open. He drags her out. This time he doesn't bother slinging her over his shoulder. He just grabs the tape between her hands and drags her along behind him. She notices a large pile of rusted junk, another El Camino up on blocks, and a tire swing hanging from a dead-looking tree.

"We gotta get inside so I can change my pants," he says. Then he turns to a skeletal dog skulking around the yard and barks at it.

The dog runs up to Amber and begins licking her face and lips. She wants to puke. The dog's breath smells horrible.

Instead, she screams, "Jim Morrison!"

"You gotta stop doing that, Amber." Vincent drags her up the stairs, the cement scraping against the backs of her calves, and searches through the myriad keys on his ring until he finds the one that fits the door. He opens the door and drags her in behind him. Once in the house, he grabs the tape tightly and slings her into the middle of the floor of a dimly lit room. Amber looks around but the room is mostly bare. There are a lot of pictures on the wall of a trashy-looking woman with very tan skin and blond starchy hair that fills most of the frame. The woman looks drunk or possibly drugged, both in her heavily shadowed, half-open eyes and in her positioning. Like she's getting ready to fall out of whatever chair the photographer put her on. Vincent pulls a chair up beside Amber and slides his knife out, playing with it.

"See them pictures on the wall?"

Amber nods.

"That's Wanda. She was perfection. She stayed around a pretty long time. She had real stamina. I was never, never too severe to her."

Amber continues to study the pictures. As she does, she realizes they are not all the same woman. They can't be. They all have the hair and the tan but some of them are fat and some of them are thin. Some look like teenagers while others look ready for a nursing home.

"She was always faithful," he says. "It wasn't easy, bein' with someone in my line of work."

"What's that?"

"I worked in the restaurant industry."

Amber looks at him, trying to make eye contact. He looks familiar.

"Pizza," he says, and she knows who it is.

"Vinnie's."

"Yep. Best pizza in Celine. Don't tell me you're a Tony's person."

She shakes her head. She would never tell him that. It's the first time he seems human to her.

"Yeah, she had to put up with all kinds of crazy hours. Tony was always tryin' to steal her away."

For a brief moment, Amber thinks about the seedy underbelly

of pizzerias. She almost laughs. She focuses and tries not to think about the names.

"What happened to her?" Amber asks, trying to somehow connect to this lunatic as a person.

"She passed."

"How?"

This makes him explode. He stands up, knocking the chair back. "It don't make no fuckin' diff'rence *how*! She passed! Okay!"

"David Bowie!"

This sends him even further into his rage. He throws himself on her, covering her in his cloying scent now mixed with the smell of old coffee. His breath is harsh against her ears. "You gotta stop sayin' them names." He gets up on his knees, straddling her. He lifts her shirt and darts the knife's tip across a few inches of her stomach. It hurts but the only thing she can do is squirm against his immovable mass. "You gotta stop sayin' them names or I'm gonna cut you again and again. And if I cut you so many times you ain't gonna be pretty to me no more and when you ain't pretty no more you won't be no use to me at all. So the only name you're gonna say is mine, 'Vincent Severity.' Got that?!"

She tries to nod but starts crying instead. "I don't think I can." How can she not say the names? If she doesn't say the names then the plague gods are going to rain down on them.

"You'll try," he says. "If you don't try, you're gonna get cut a lot. Do you understand that?"

This time she nods.

"See that woman there on the wall?"

Amber nods again.

"That's Wanda. You wanna know what you got in common?"

She isn't even going to tell him he has just told her about Wanda.

This time he doesn't even wait for her to respond before saying, "The chin. You both have the same chin." He gets back up and paces around the room. "When I lost her I thought I'd lost everything and then I seen you one day in the parlor. You couldn'ta been more than ten at the time but you better believe how I noticed your chin and I thought to myself, 'She could be Wanda.' She's got that chin and maybe that's the closest thing I'll ever find. And I waited. I waited 'cause there ain't really ever been a ten-year-old yet that's turned me on and I waited 'cause I thought I might find somebody closer but nobody ever came along and I waited 'cause Wanda was still alive.

Take off your clothes. I'm gonna make you pretty."

"I can't," she says. "My hands are tied."

"And they'll stay tied!" he screams. Then he's on her again, his knife cutting through her layers of clothes. He does it with such harsh quickness she feels for sure he's going to cut her. With just her panties on he looks down at her and breathes appreciatively.

"Yeah, you got a real nice body," he says. "But you're too pale. Wanda wasn't pale. You look like a fuckin' corpse. You almost match your undies, you're so white." Now he cuts those off too and stands back up. "But I knew you was white. So I got somethin' to show ya."

He grabs her by the hair and pulls her to her feet. He lifts her by the hips and carries her toward the back of the house, into what would probably have been a family room if there was any furniture in it. In the far wall is a door that looks like it belongs in a slaughter-house or a prison. Heavy and metal, with no window and a slide-action bolt. He sits her down to open the door. It doesn't open in or out, it slides into the wall.

Amber is blinded by the exposed room. It's like looking directly at the sun, it's so bright. She wants to shield her eyes but can't raise her arms.

"Elliot Smith!"

He scratches the knife across her lower back. She feels the sting-ing burn and wishes she could keep her mouth closed.

"Say it," he seethes into her ear. "Say it."

"Vincent Severity!" she shouts. But it's half-hearted. It isn't *his* name that stops the plague gods. Shouting his name doesn't make her feel good on the inside. It makes her feel tainted.

"See that?" he says. "See how much I love you? You know how long I spent makin' this room? Makin' it just for you. Them's fifty sun lamps up there on the ceilin' all ready to make you as tan as my Wanda. Know how long it took to wire all that shit up? Get on in there."

He shoves her into the room and points the knife between her legs. "And Wanda never had no landin' strip either. Nope. She liked a big ole bush. So we'll have to fix that up to." Then he slams the door and shoots the bolt into place.

She collapses into the middle of the floor, thinking she has never felt so lost, alone, and humiliated. Drowning in doom on the surface of the sun. She wonders how crazy Vincent really is. And she wonders how she's going to get out. The room is very hot and she feels the sweat that has never stopped continue to pour out of her.

6

She has no idea how long she's been in the room. The lights come on and go off at irregular intervals, Vincent controlling them with an outside switch. Although Amber figures he is in a hurry to make her tan, presumably so he can fuck her and convince himself he is fucking Wanda, he apparently does not want her to get sunburned. Over time, she feels her skin grow warm and taut. Sometimes he comes in and throws bite-size food at her as hard as he can. She never eats it in front of him. But when he leaves the room, she crawls around and gobbles it up, eating it like a wild and starving animal which, in a sense, she has become.

She can't stop shouting the names and she has many small cuts to prove it. And when he turns on the lights and she starts to sweat, the sweat runs into the cuts and she has to toss around on the floor because she can't wipe it away with her hand. Somewhere along the line the duct tape was replaced with actual hand and ankle cuffs. For a long time, the thought of escaping the tape had been the only thing keeping her from giving up all hope. Now she doesn't even have that to look forward to.

She hates the sight of Vincent and can't stand to say his name. Every day, sometimes a few times a day, he comes in—sliding the door open and squinting against the harsh light and he reaches behind himself, his hand first missing the door handle before finally seizing it and pulling it just closed enough so she can't go charging out. And he shouts at her while the pelted food smacks against her burning skin, "You ain't tan! You ain't nearly tan enough!"

She could have told him that girls like her don't typically tan—they redden. And then the red goes away and they are as pale as they ever were. But Vincent carries on with his savage dream.

In the room, Amber has a lot of time to think and, naturally, everything she thinks about involves her escape. One day, Vincent had come into the bright room and dragged her into the bathroom where he held her head over the bathtub and bleached her dark hair. He had to lean over her, against her, to do it, and she could feel his hardness through his jeans. That was when she realized she was becoming more attractive to him and it scared the hell out of her more than anything else he had done so far.

7

She feels a sense of being out of control, like she's racing toward something she can't stop. She figures she only has a couple of days. A couple of days until she is just another Wanda. Maybe that will buy her a certain amount of freedom but she can't think of what she'll have to do for that. The thought of Vincent touching her, let alone fucking her, makes her physically ill. What will he do the first time he rapes her and she vomits all over him? She knows the answer to this. His name is Vincent Severity. He does very severe things. He's a very severe man.

He'll do something very severe.

He might even kill her.

After all, the world is full of Wandas. All they need is a lot of tanning and a lot of bleach and a lot of hairspray and anyone can become a Wanda.

Lately, he's been acting crazier than usual. She hears him in the other room, even through the heavy metal door. He yells things. Crazy incoherent things. He throws and breaks things. When he comes into the tanning room, he's pale and sick looking.

She crouches naked in her corner as he yells and slams around the other room.

She watches a maggot cross the floor. She wonders if the people of Scruffington are still quarantined but doesn't dare ask him about that. That feels like another world to her anyway. To be a Wanda is to be a part of Vincent Severity and nobody else.

"Wayne Coyne!" she shouts and bites her tongue. She's been biting her tongue a lot lately.

The maggot continues to cross the floor. Maggots are so sick and gross. She wonders if anyone is searching for her. She wonders if people just think she has run off. As far as she knows, she has never given them a reason to think this.

The maggot inches sickly, grossly closer. She reaches out her foot and squashes it beneath her big toe. The feel of it makes her gag.

The door to the room bangs open.

Vincent stands there, his eyes swirling with rage. His dog is beside him. At first, Amber thinks it's standing on its own and then she realizes he's holding it by the collar and the dog is limp. He holds the knife in the other hand. He is not wearing a shirt. His chest is hairy; the rest of his skin is pale and covered in sweat. His plastic hair is messed up. This scares Amber. She doesn't know why but she feels like, once he lets his appearance slide, Vincent is capable of doing just about anything.

"Thurston Moore!" She bites her tongue again and curls into herself.

Vincent rushes over, dragging the dog with her. He slices at her arm.

"Say it! Say it! Say it!"

"Vincent Severity! Vincent Severity! Vincent Severity!"

"Yeah, bitchface, that's better."

He steps back from her and tucks the knife into the back of his pants. He grabs his crotch with his right hand and shifts his cock around. She can see it outlined in those tight blue jeans. He probably isn't wearing any underwear. Gross.

"Want you to see what you done with your shoutin'. You done kilt Boy."

He pulls his left arm up and the dog goes with it. He shakes it in front of her. Some maggots fall off and onto the floor.

"He ain't never gonna be the same."

Amber wants to run but she's backed into a corner. She wants to kick Vincent's face away from hers and run but she's wearing the ankle cuffs and knows she will not get very far, even if he is sick. She starts crying. She can't help it.

"Stop cryin'! I should be the one cryin'! I'm the one just lost his dog!"

Two or three of the maggots are crawling up her calf. She can feel them but doesn't want to look at them because she's afraid that will make her puke.

"You need to say your goodbyes." He squats down, takes the dead dog's head in between his hands and forces it up to her face.

"Boy loves kisses," he says. Now he's rubbing the moist nose and stinking lips against her face, against her mouth. She can feel the maggots crawling around the dog's teeth, pressing against her lips. "Yeah, give old Boy some kisses. Let him get one last taste of ya."

She looks at Vincent, the sweat running down his plastic skin. She looks at the dog, its eyes open and all milked over. Now she sees the dog is *covered* in maggots. They're squirming all over its hide. And

Vincent's forcing the maggots and the stink into her hose, into her mouth, and she thinks she's finally losing it. A person can't be subjected to this and then expect to come back.

She vomits.

Throws up all over the dog. The puke runs down and covers Vincent's hands.

And he's using the dog's head to hit her in the face and shoulders, rubbing her puke back onto her.

She continues to cry and murmurs, "Daniel Johnston."

"You'll never learn. You'll never learn! You'll NEVER LEARN!"

He stands up, leaving the dog's crawling carcass on her body, and heads for the open door. In the doorway, he braces himself, vomits, and looks back over his shoulder. "Say it!"

"Vincent Severity!" A shout from a burning throat.

She wishes she was dead.

She hopes he'll forget to shut the door but he doesn't. It slams shut and she hears the bolt slide into place and then the lights cut off.

She doesn't know if it's good to not be able to see the dog or bad to not know where the maggots are.

8

Since being taken prisoner, she has grown very adept at working with her hands behind her back. Once she adjusted to having them there, her whole range of movement consisting merely of the expanse of her buttocks, she learned to use them quite well. Not a second has passed when she hasn't thought of escape. When Vincent comes in, he can't see her. She has watched him from her place on the floor. She has watched him open the door, squint and blink. The next time he comes in, she thinks, she'll go for it. The lights flick on. It doesn't take them long to heat up. She looks toward the pile of Boy on the floor. What used to be Boy. Oh God, she thinks. Then blurts, "Trent Reznor!" The dog has been reduced to a pile of bones. The maggots cling to the bones, make them wriggle and look alive. The maggots spread out all over the floor. Some of them are on her. She closes her eyes against the heat, against the sight of all those maggots. She thinks she might not be the only one in trouble.

Vincent enters suddenly, surprising her just enough to throw her finely honed design all out of whack. He slides the door open and stands there wearing only his stained white briefs. He's dragging a television behind him. The television is on a cheap metal stand. The kind with wheels. The kind usually found in the seediest motel rooms.

He looks sick and wasted away.

"The whole world's gone to hell," he says. "You ain't Wanda. Wanda ain't never comin' back."

He flips the television on. The picture rolls and then comes in staticky. It looks like the news. He crosses the room toward her. As he gets closer, she can see his skin bulging and twitching and she imagines him filled with maggots.

"They're callin' 'em slags," he says. "They say they're everwhere."

He grabs her from behind the neck and pulls her out into the middle of the floor, kicking the bones of Boy away.

Amber watches the television and realizes not even the names could keep the plague gods away.

Vincent kicks her knees out from under her and forces her onto the floor, onto her stomach. She thinks he's going to kill her and thinks she's blown her chance.

He circles behind her.

"You ain't Wanda. You ain't never gonna be Wanda. First you kilt Boy and now you're killin' the world."

He drops to his knees behind her and she hears his underwear slide down his thighs.

She watches the television.

The dour newsman drones: "New York. Boston. Chicago. Miami. Atlanta." He continues reading off his list of major cities. He looks tired and gray and Amber hopes it's just the television making him look that way. Vincent is pressing his cock between her legs. He's spitting in his hand for lubrication. He's leaning with one hand pressed on her ass cheek. She thinks about fighting back but, as she continues to pay attention to the television, she continues to wonder if there is even a point in fighting back.

"Los Angeles. Portland. All under quarantine. All infected. The CDC and the government have both advised you to stay in your homes. If you see any signs of slags, these maggot-like organisms, in your saliva, vomit, stool, or discharge, do not go to the hospital. I repeat: DO NOT GO TO THE HOSPITALS. They are all full and desperately understaffed. They will not be able to help you. You will only spread the infection."

Vincent presses against her. It hurts. She grits her teeth. She opens up and he keeps going.

"No hope," he says. "No hope at all."

And he thrusts into her, slowly, tediously, painfully.

On the television, the anchorman says, "Really, what's the fucking point to all of this?" And then the television cuts to video footage. Traffic jams. Fires. People dead in the street. Armies in hazmat suits mowing crowds down with flamethrowers.

Vincent wraps his hands around her arms and pumps harder.

The television cuts back to the anchorman. His nose is bleeding and he looks even more disheveled. He's reading from a piece of paper: "If you are in the southwestern Ohio viewing area and you are not yet infected, I repeat: NOT YET INFECTED, then you are ordered by the power of the United States government to report to Hollow City. You are needed . . ."

Vincent lets out a growl and she feels him come into her and she wonders if she's infected. If Vincent is infected, it seems like she should be.

He pulls out of her and she can feel the slags wriggling around deep inside her bowels.

"I have to go," she says to no one in particular. She rolls over on her back, sits up on her ass, and presses her thighs together. She can feel the slags moving beneath her.

"You're sure as hell infected now."

He's standing there in front of her, the television flickering against his waxy skin. He's holding his penis in his hand and working it until it softens. She can see the slags peeking out the tip, crawling in and out, around the head. He pulls his underwear up and smacks her in the face. He drags her back to the corner and shoves her face in it.

"Don't move from there. HEAR ME! I need to figger some things out." He coughs and spits on the back of her head.

"Bruce Dickinson," she mumbles.

She hears him grab his knife from the top of the television and he slices her with it.

"SAY IT! SAY IT! SAY IT!" he shouts before having another coughing fit.

"Vincent Severity!" she yells.

"That's fuckin' right."

He grabs the television and throws it at her before leaving the room. It smashes on the floor at least two feet before her.

The lights go off and she knows the next time he enters the room has to be it. If he ever enters the room again. If not . . .

What if he dies while he's out there?

No choice. She has no choice.

9

Time seems strange. She thinks maybe he really isn't coming back or maybe it's just her mind playing tricks on her. He's already fucked her, so what is the point in him coming back? It was a desperation fuck. She knows this. He didn't delude himself into thinking he was fucking Wanda. It was just something to do before he died.

Before he died.

Leaving her in this room with the bones of a dead dog and the slags covering the wall.

The light comes on and she gets her hopes up.

10

She feels dead with hunger when the door actually opens. Maybe it won't be him. Maybe it will be someone there to rescue her.

No.

It's him.

Go for the eyes, she thinks. That has been her mantra ever since realizing what she planned to do.

He reaches down to clasp the door handle and she knows if he actually closes the door then it's all over. She will never make it out alive. She wants to remain silent. She's crouched right beside the door. She wants to not blow her cover until she is right up on him but she blurts "Syd Barrett!" and then she has to act. She springs at him, standing right there beside her, and rams her head into what's left of his face.

He slashes out with the knife, catching her just below her ribs. It goes in deeper than the other ones had. Those had been warning, cautionary cuts. *Keep him from the door,* she thinks, *and go for the eyes. Go for the eyes.*

He reaches out for her but maybe his eyes have not fully adjusted to the light because he can't grab her. She throws her body crossways into his knees and feels the blade come down hard into her ass. Already, she is covered in blood. She has to move before he has the chance to stab again. He's bent over. She raises her head as fast as she can, praying she doesn't run it into the knife. The back of her skull connects with his nose and she hears a popping noise, feels the slags squirming against her scalp.

"Robert Smith!" she shouts. Then she falls onto her hands and sweeps her legs around behind his, dropping him to the ground.

"Stop sayin' those fuckin names!" he shouts, swinging his arm out with the knife but now he's on the squirming floor and she is standing up. She eyes the distance, sits down perpendicularly to him, brings her ankles together, raises them and brings the heavy cuffs down onto his left kneecap, shattering it.

She wants to go for the eyes but he has the knife.

And he's trying to stand up. If it weren't for the damn ankle cuffs she could just run and she's pretty sure she could outrun him. She can't let him stand up. She leaps across him, bounding from her place on the ground, and brings both her knees down into his other knee.

He swings the knife down toward her back but she's already moving away from him and the blade slices rather than plunges. Her organs are grateful.

She has visualized so much of this in her head. What he would do with the knife, how she could maneuver in her restrained fashion, that it feels almost like she's fighting something she's practiced before.

He swings out with the knife again and she raises the cuffs behind her enough to snag the point in one of the few chain links. Quickly jerking her wrists, the knife falls from his hand and she throws herself on it.

He still has upper body strength, she reminds herself, thinking of that bullish head on those bullish shoulders. But he's weakened so much. Parts of his skin have been eaten away.

He sits up and pushes her back, trying to get her off the knife but she already has it in her hands. His face is a mass of blood from his exploded nose. She turns with her back toward him, still on her knees, and thrusts herself backward, careful not to let go of the blade's handle as it plunges into his flesh. The knife hits to the right of his bellybutton, barely missing the huge, transplanted nipple.

Using his still considerable arm strength, he grabs her around the neck, squeezing brutally and lifting her up. She manages to plant her feet on the floor and give another great thrust, this time aiming the knife near his head. His hands, slick with blood, slip, and she buries the knife in his left eye. He squeals in pain and clamps his teeth on her lower buttock.

Knowing she is in position, she mentally gauges where his right eye would be from the position of her hands. She's surprised she hasn't penetrated the brain. His teeth grind against her flesh.

She savagely stabs the knife downward, feels it punch into his eye, and screams, "John Lennon!"

This is her time to leave, while he is blinded, while those powerful arms are off her and reaching for his wounded head. She stands up, continuing to clutch the knife, and begins hopping toward the door. He drags himself through his expanding pool of blood and slags, almost catching her, snarling, "Stop sayin' those stupid fuckin' names!"

Crossing the threshold, she clasps the large handle of the iron door and, looking down at him, shouts a little rhyme she has worked on in the madness of her confines, "Vincent Severity isn't so severe. With both his eyes gone he's really quite dear!" before slamming the door and searching the house for the keys to the cuffs.

11

She finds the keys. They're hanging right next to the front door. If she hadn't become so used to doing things with her hands behind her back, she never would have been able to get them unlocked. It's painful. The cuffs dig into the flesh of her arms but she's lost so much weight she's able to slide them up, manipulate them so she can fit the key into the hole and slowly turn. She rummages in his closet for some clothes. She thinks about looking for some gas to burn his whole fucking house down. But when she thinks about the slags slowly consuming him, she realizes she likes that idea better. She takes the keys to the El Camino and walks outside.

She has the desire to shout a name but she quickly realizes there isn't a name in the world that can undo this kind of damage. The plague gods have found her but, miraculously, she feels like she is not infected.

She climbs in the car and starts toward Hollow City. Past the destroyed and burning buildings. The trees stripped bare. The mounds of burning dead piled up outside of towns. Past all of this.

On her way to Hollow City.

PART THREE

CORPSE MOUNTAIN

1

Two men sit in an El Camino and watch Reverend Hacksaw set fire to the Baptist church. The El Camino is nearly totaled. It came barreling into their trailer about three days ago. The woman driving it was dead. Hence, the accident. It still ran okay and they decided it was theirs. They didn't figure there would be much in the way of an insurance settlement and thought they needed some form of repayment.

The dead woman is still in the car.

"What do you think he's doing?" Rambo asks.

"Fuck if I know," Cobra says.

2

Until a week ago they had been John and Larry. Larry said, "Fuck it. If God is dead then I don't need to use my God given name anymore."

"What should we call you now?"

"Rambo."

"Fuck yeah. Call me Cobra."

They toasted over goblets of gasoline and went to see how Will was doing with the robots. Will became Commando. Commando thought he knew two things. One: drinking out of goblets was medieval and badass. Two: Robots could save the world.

3

"That's a fuck ton of gasoline that guy with hair is using," Cobra says.

Rambo says, "Yep, he's got gasoline and legs."

It's a pointless observation. The church is really burning now. The Reverend says something about building a mountain to God and throws himself into the fire.

Rambo forgets where he is, forgets what he's watching, and chalks it up to the gasoline intake or maybe thinks he has a slag stuck somewhere in his head.

The sky is blue.

The smoke is black and covering it up.

Cobra has two eyes and a unibrow and for a second Rambo wants to punch him in the face to make the unibrow separate in two.

"Smells like burning," he says.

Cobra coughs and asks if he wants to go to the refrigerator graveyard and see if Commando's there.

Rambo can't remember where the refrigerator graveyard is but says okay and that he thinks the El Camino is sick and he's pretty sure there's a dead woman filled with slags in the bed of it.

Cobra tells him the world is mostly water and evil anyway and they pull away, chugging gasoline straight from the plastic milk jug.

Neither one of them can remember what Commando said about goblets. He might have been talking about goblins.

4

Five hours later they finally reach the refrigerator graveyard. During this time they pass the burning church several times. Sometimes Rambo points out that the church is burning. Sometimes it's Cobra.

It's dark by the time they get to the refrigerator graveyard. It helps that it's the only remaining place in town that has electricity. The front of the graveyard, which is actually called Flemion's Scrap and Metal, is just a trailer. Out back, stadium lights shine on junked cars, washing machines, dryers, old school buses, and random piles of miscellany. But, perhaps oddly, the most predominate things are refrigerators. They line a central walkway. They are in virtually every color, some loud and vibrant and others more muted.

Neither Cobra nor Rambo can remember seeing a refrigerator that was anything other than white or black in a house or trailer.

"Where the fuck you guys been?" Commando asks. He sounds mad a lot.

Rambo says, "Somebody burnt down the church."

Cobra says, "Like five times."

Rambo says, "How are the robots coming?"

"You get the shit I asked for?"

"Uh," Cobra says. "We got a car with a dead girl in the back and the Reverend burned down the church."

"Burned down himself too."

"I sent you specifically to the hardware store. Please tell me you went to the hardware store."

"We couldn't find the hardware store," Cobra says.

"Did you get more gas?"

"For the car? Yeah."

Commando punches Cobra in the stomach. Cobra drops to the ground and vomits. Gasoline fumes waft from him.

"For the generators, fucker. How do you think the lights stay on here?"

Cobra can't say anything. He continues to writhe around on the ground and flap his arms.

"We thought everything runs on magic. That's what you said."

"No." Commando shakes his head. "That is not what I said."

"Oh." Rambo looks up at one of the bright stadium lights and continues to stare. First the light is white and then blue and then orange and then pink and then they're spinning all around and he stops thinking or seeing.

5

What Commando actually told them was a version of what his grandfather had told him a very long time ago. Commando couldn't help but think his grandfather knew the slags were coming. Even though he never lived to see it, he predicted something like this was going to happen.

He said somewhere out in space was a place called the Garbage Planet. That probably wasn't its real name, the smart name, but it was out there. On Garbage Planet, people found a use for waste. He said it was evolution. He said they were training it. That's what recycling was. It was our attempt to train garbage to be something else. That's why he opened the scrap yard. So he could surround himself with garbage and things people just didn't want anymore. On Garbage Planet, he would have been a king. This was mostly metal garbage he collected. Expensive stuff. It was worthless to most people because they didn't want it anymore, but if you added up what people had originally paid for this stuff, he would have been a millionaire.

The problem with Garbage Planet was, once the garbage evolved, it could first live alongside humans and then it would overtake them. People and trash would become so indistinguishable nobody would be able to tell which was which. Then the only things able to live would be the maggots and the roaches and the parasites. And they didn't know how to do anything but expand and expand and expand and take over as many hosts as possible. He said eventually they would start taking over whole planets. And that was how he said we'd know when we were fully evolved. Humans, he said, aren't really given to suicide and it would take something apocalyptic to make the planet remotely livable, to get rid of the excess humans.

Commando was too young to know what to believe but now he believed. He believed the slags' arrival heralded the shift in evolution. They'd entered the next phase. Even their biology had changed. It would take some sort of symbiotic relationship with the garbage surrounding him if he wanted to survive.

6

Rambo wakes up in roughly the same spot where he collapsed. He stands up and nudges Cobra with his foot. Maybe they can sneak out before Commando knows they're awake. Maybe they can drive into town and see if there's anybody left who has anything left inside. Most people have gone crazy. He wants to do more than nudge Cobra. He wants to kick him and just keep on kicking.

Cobra flaps his hands and says he's awake, that his eyes are out of his head.

Rambo has to piss and thinks about pissing on Cobra. His mouth tastes like gasoline. His stomach is burning. He might be blind in his left eye.

Cobra stands up very slowly.

Commando storms from the back of the trailer and into the scrap yard. He holds a piece of paper and something Rambo thinks is a stapler only he's pretty sure it's called a slambox.

"You guys are going back into town. This time I made a list." He shakes the piece of paper in his left hand, slaps it to Cobra's cheek, and staples it there. Cobra says "ow" once but doesn't make any attempt to stop him.

"Have you guys pissed yet?" Commando says.

"No, but I really have to," Rambo says.

"Go use the jugs over there." He points to a place in front of a fluorescent orange refrigerator. "Make sure you take plenty of gas with you."

7

They walk out front to the El Camino. Cobra is breathing very heavily. He says it feels like something is in his stomach. Rambo tells him he's probably growing a second skull. Cobra says he feels like there's something on his face. Rambo checks and says there is. It's a list.

The list says:
HAMMERS
WRENCHES
SCREWDRIVERS
SCREWS
NAILS
BOLT CUTTERS
YOU GUYS ARE BOTH CUNTFACED ASSHOLES
Rambo says he doesn't like the tone of it but they should probably leave it there.

Standing beside the car, looking into the back of it, is a man in a black robe. Cobra and Rambo stop about ten feet away and stare. Cobra strokes the piece of paper on his face.

"Excuse me," the man says. "Is that a dead person in the back of your car?"

Cobra and Rambo continue to stare. Rambo thinks there was a time when the answer to that question should have been 'no' but he's not so sure how to answer it now.

The man, maybe thinking Rambo and Cobra can't hear him, walks toward them. He holds out a bony hand.

"I'm Gravedigger John."

Rambo wonders if that's his God given name and thinks maybe he should change it to 'Slappy'.

"I just peed in a jug," Rambo says.

"I've got a lower skull." Cobra points to his stomach.

"Those both sound like excellent and wonderful things, gentlemen, but what I'm here for is to see if I can't take that corpse off your hands. It's a donation, I want you to understand, to God's Mountaineers."

Rambo thinks that sounds fun. He says, "Cave hat," and makes a chopping motion with his arm.

"Of course. Of course!" Gravedigger John pats him on the arm. "I'll just get that all loaded up."

Commando storms out from the front of the trailer.

Rambo turns and shouts, "This is Slappy!"

"I know who the hell it is," Commando says. "What the hell you want, John?"

"Your friends here have a dead body in the back of their truck or car or . . . whatever it is. I've joined an organization called God's Mountaineers." He points to a large truck idling on the side of the road. It's a pick-up truck with giant pieces of plywood rising from the bed. A childish mountain ascending into a radiant cross is sloppily spray painted in yellow on the side of the plywood.

"I don't see what that has to do with dead bodies."

"Since we cannot give everyone a proper burial, we have decided to place them in a communal grave. A mountain in the center of town so that we may return to the god who has stricken us down and beg his forgiveness. Maybe then this horrible plague will leave us in peace."

"Aren't you afraid of slags?"

"I think if they really wanted me, they would have taken me by now. This would be a great act of charity, Mr. Flemian. Each corpse gets us that much closer to God."

"Take it. I don't care. Say, would you mind helping me out?"

"Anything for a philanthropist such as yourself."

"Will you let these boys follow you to the hardware store? Their brains are ate up with slags. There's a list stapled to that one's face. Could you help them pick up what's on the list and send them back?"

"Very well," Gravedigger John says. "They can just leave the body in the trunk until we get into town."

Commando turns to walk away and spins back around. "You picked up any reports?"

Gravedigger John nods his head. His good-natured smile drops for just a moment.

"And?"

"They seem to be getting bigger. Some of them are as big as we are."

"Where?"
"The coasts mostly."
"How long?"
"A week at the most."
"Thanks."
"God bless."

8

The drive to town is treacherous. Rambo closes his bad eye and tries to focus as best he can. Cobra rubs his stomach and wonders what he's going to name the new person he's certain is growing there. They follow Gravedigger John as best as possible. One of the El Camino's axles must be bent or something because the car goes up and down, up and down. Cobra says he feels sick and Rambo stops the car so he can vomit out the window.

"How'd it look," Rambo asks.

"Full," Cobra says.

Rambo assumes this means full of slags. He passes the jug of gasoline to Cobra and he pounds it. They forget where they are, what they're doing. The big truck with all the corpses in the back honks its horn. Rambo remembers they're supposed to be following it.

They reach town and stop in front of the hardware store. Cobra writhes on the passenger side. Slappy gets out of his truck and comes around to the passenger side. He plucks the piece of paper from Cobra's face and tells the boys they should put the woman in the back of their car into his truck while he's in the store. Cobra doesn't listen to him. He just continues to writhe around on the seat. Rambo gets out of the car and hopes the slags have eaten most of the woman away. He feels tired. Tired all the time. And his muscles feel full of lead. He lets down the tailgate and drags the woman by her feet. It looks like she might have been decent looking at one point in time. Maybe when she had her whole face. Slags cover her body but they're not the big kind of slags. Rambo holds out his finger to one of them to see if it tries to bite it but it shrivels away. He begins to walk back to the driver's side of the car and then remembers he's supposed to move the woman. He pulls her the rest of the way out in one swift motion and then walks as fast as he can to Slappy's truck. He tosses the woman in and stands for a couple of seconds, staring in awe at the mass of bodies in the back of the truck.

He remembers a church in town and remembers that sometimes it used to give him peace but when he walks a little way down the street to see if he can see it, there is just a pile of smoldering ash lined with dead bodies. The embers are cooking the bodies and he thinks it smells really good. His stomach rumbles. He wonders why someone has decided to cook so many dead bodies. Maybe they're going to offer them to the slags when they finally come. Cooked meat always tastes better than raw.

Standing there in the street in the middle of the dead town with everyone either dead or hiding in their locked-up homes gives Rambo the creeps. He walks back to the El Camino, hops in, and speeds away.

When he looks to his right, he's startled to see Cobra there. Cobra isn't moving. Some kind of yellow-tinged foam is oozing from the corner of his mouth. Rambo pokes his finger into it and tastes it. Tastes like gasoline and something else, maybe battery acid. He pulls away from the curb. He turns the radio on and up. It's just static bursting through the speakers but Rambo pretends it's a song called "In the Hall of the Abortion King" that he really liked before the radio went crackly.

9

In the scrap yard, there's a dirty mirror propped up against a sky blue refrigerator. Commando looks in the mirror and tries to think about what his grandfather told him about the Garbage Planet. It wasn't just the one time he had told him about this kind of thing. The old man would go on and on about it. Commando had ideas. He had all kinds of ideas. But he feels like these ideas aren't coming true. What his grandfather described was some kind of intuitive science, something that couldn't be found out by any scientist or hiding in the pages of a book. What his grandfather described was something that could only be felt in the bones and the skin and, if he had one, the soul. Commando feels this knowledge reaching out for him. But there's still something he feels like he isn't hearing.

Take, for instance, the robots. Commando feels robots can save the world. But right now, he only has two piles of scrap metal. It was after having the idea about the robots he came to the realization he didn't have a clue how the hell he'd build one. He needed the voices reaching out for him to instruct him, guide him. The best way to hear them, he thought, was to install an antenna. He found a rusty awl on the ground and got a starter hole going, trying to center it on the top of his head. Then he found an old stainless steel car antenna and unscrewed it from the car.

Now he stands in front of the mirror and screws the antenna into his skull. There seems to be a profuse amount of blood but what was the worst that could happen? He figures if he's meant to die then he's going to die. The slags are a definite sign, if not a God given one, that people are being placed on sides. The living and the dead. If he's meant to live, if he's one of the chosen, then he's going to live. Nothing could stop him.

He nearly blacks out installing the antenna, takes a couple of deep breaths, and wanders around the scrap yard trying to pick up a signal.

It's late afternoon when he hears a car pulling up out front. He hopes Rambo and Cobra have brought him everything he asked for. He has an idea about the robots. Building them isn't going to be the hard part. It's the animating them that will give him problems. But that spooky knowledge that was only there in bits and pieces, the knowledge that made him think it was a good idea for he and his partners to drink gasoline, showed him the reason for this. He feels more alive than he has in weeks.

10

Commando's surprised to see it's Gravedigger John and not Cobra and Rambo and then he isn't surprised at all. It isn't dark yet and he hasn't turned on the lights. Not once on their night prowls, at least since they'd upped their intake of gasoline, had they been able to find the scrap yard.

John steps from the cab of the truck carrying an olive green canvas army sack with lots of odd shapes bulging from it. He smiles and raises his free hand. As he draws closer to Commando, he glances up at his new antenna and says, "Them boys ran off before I could give them your tools. Wasn't sure how much you needed them so I figured I'd drop them off before my next corpse run."

"Yeah. They're fucking idiots. How's it going?"

"How's what going?"

"The collecting."

"Pretty good. We should be about where we want to be by the

end of the week. It's pretty much just me doing the collecting but we have a few builders helping out. You really should consider being a Mountaineer. I find it rewarding."

"How many?"

"How many corpses?"

"How many Mountaineers?"

"About six."

Commando thinks this is a lie. "Any women?"

"No."

Commando thinks this is a lie too. He wonders if John is protecting them for their benefit or if he's protecting them because he wants to keep them as sex slaves.

"And you're planning on . . . making a mountain out of the corpses?"

"That's right."

Commando touches his forehead, maybe looking for an answer from space. "Why?"

"Because I feel like that's what God wants."

"Intuitive knowledge."

"Pardon?"

"I think you're talking about intuitive knowledge. You hear a voice in your head, right?"

"Well, it's more like something I feel in my soul."

"I hear that voice too, sometimes. It wants me to build robots."

"Robots?"

"That's right."

"Well, if that's what you think you have to do. Personally, I feel like your time would best be spent among the Mountaineers, in a community, building a future."

"Robots. My time is best spent making robots." Commando is suddenly angry. He feels like grabbing Gravedigger John and shaking him, telling him there is no God, that the voice he hears is wrong. It lacks clarity and focus. "You need to install yourself one of these!" He points to the antenna in his head, flicks it, and feels a metallic twinge rattle through his skull and jaw bones.

John is already backing away. "Think about what I said. You'll always have a place with the Mountaineers!" He's climbing into his idling truck and pulling back out onto the road. Commando sees his pious smiling face in his head, probably brought to him by the antenna, and he thinks he'll give it some time. If the robots don't work, maybe he'll see about becoming a Mountaineer, but he can't see anything dumber or more ghoulish than building a mountain of corpses.

He goes into the trailer, rinses out a goblet, and drinks some Gatorade. The green kind.

11

It's just after dark and Rambo is driving toward the light. He throws occasional glances toward Cobra. Slags have begun crawling out of his mouth. Rambo thinks he should scream but his throat won't make the sound and he's secretly hoping the slags will bring the skull or the baby or the goblin Cobra had growing in him out so he could see it. He doesn't want to have to cut him open but he will. Unless he forgets. He thinks he should write it down. He wishes he had a slambox so he could put it on his face.

He almost runs the El Camino into the trailer but slams on the brakes just in time. He wants to get away from Cobra and he throws the door open and goes spinning out into the humid night and then he tries to stand still but his body and his brain just keep spinning and spinning and then he's lying in the gravel with Commando looking down at him. Commando has something on his head and Rambo thinks it makes him look like a unicorn.

"Unicorn!" He points at Commando's antenna. Commando kicks him in the side.

"You guys forget something?"

"Rambo had a baby. Somebody burnt down the church. The town is dead."

"The hardware store?"

"Huh?"

"It's okay. Gravedigger John brought them. I'm glad I could count on you. Where's Cobra?"

Rambo's mouth opens and some weird keening sound comes from it.

"Please stop," Commando says.

Rambo continues, only louder.

"Please stop making that sound."

Commando covers his ears with his hands and walks over to the car, leaving Rambo to lie on the ground. He looks into the passenger side and says, "Fuck fuck fuck fuck fuck!"

12

At their best, humans are pure inside.

Garbage Planet is toxic.

Space is toxic.

Space is toxic and it rains down slags onto the earth.

The slags want humans because they are, at their best, pure inside.

Humans need to become toxic to keep the slags away.

They need to be garbage on the outside and toxic on the inside.

Hence, the robots.

The antenna tells him this.

13

Rambo rolls over and Cobra is lying next to him in the gravel. Only this isn't the gravel where he collapsed whenever. This is the gravel of the scrap yard. He doesn't remember wandering back here. Cobra smells really bad and he's missing his face. What happened to Cobra's face? Rambo thinks about screaming again but he just wants some more gasoline. He wants to drink it and let it fill up his empty stomach until he can feel it burbling at the back of his throat.

He tries to stand up but he can't. He thinks maybe he's glued to the ground but he can vaguely see he has some sort of yellow rope around his wrists. He can't look over his bloated stomach to see his ankles. Maybe his legs have turned to lead. Maybe he will have babies out of his feet. Maybe his toes have been taken by goblins.

Commando stands above him. He's drinking something that looks like gasoline from his goblet, looking cool as hell. Commando never drinks gasoline. He usually drinks whatever that stuff is that makes you sweat paint. He's surprised by the antenna until he remembers Commando is now a unicorn. He wonders if Commando is his God given name and thinks maybe he should change it to Unicorn Skyhair.

"I don't see how you guys drink this shit." He offers the goblet to Rambo and Rambo lets him pour the gasoline down his throat.

"I grew into the ground." He belches.

"You sure did."

"Cobra's face fell off."

"It sure did."

"The world has gone bad."

Commando laughs. Throws back his head and laughs and laughs and laughs. The antenna bounces around on his head, framed by the blue sky.

Unicorn Skyhair.

Rambo laughs too.

14

Commando spends the morning gathering and shaping metal. He lays the pieces out in a row between Cobra and Rambo. Cobra's body is twitching with all the slags packing his insides and writhing beneath the skin. He thinks maybe he could still use him, but the antenna tells him this is a bad idea. He knows what he's going to have to do. He can't drink gasoline. He's tried but he just can't.

He's hungry. He hasn't had meat in weeks so maybe it won't be as hard as he thinks.

The sun is very high in the sky when he hooks the drill up to the generator and places the first piece on Rambo's forehead. He drills in the first screw and Rambo screams, wide-eyed and incomprehensible.

Maybe Rambo needs an antenna too. Maybe he needs to hear the calming space voice. The voice of knowledge and reason. The voice of intuition.

He looks for an antenna and can't find one. How did he get so lucky? This is something he's never noticed before. It bothers him that he's missed this. That he's grown up in a scrap yard and never noticed that none of the junked cars have antennas. It seems like the least important thing to take. He imagines a car, somewhere out there, covered in antennas, or perhaps made entirely of antennas.

He gives up and looks for anything long and metallic and removable.

He finds a scythe in relatively good shape and returns to Rambo.

He bores a hole in Rambo's skull, saws down the handle of the scythe and inserts it into the hole. It's a little loose so he fills the hole with glue and scrap metal shavings. Then he remembers wood is not really a conductor so he finds a massive pile of copper wire and wraps the handle with it, making sure plenty of the wire gets down into Rambo's skull.

Rambo continues to scream. Commando feeds him more gasoline.

15

Rambo tries his hardest to get up off the ground. He wants to be in the El Camino and driving around town with Cobra, feeling like the only two people alive. He likes the way the El Camino rocks up and down on the road. It makes him think of a ship. He looks at the sky and how blue it is and wonders why the sky had to kill everyone and thinks, if anything, the sky is more dangerous than the sea.

A sense of dread fills him when Unicorn Skyhair comes tromping back into his vision, holding more pieces to his puzzle of pain and working it out on Rambo's skin.

But there's a constant flow of gasoline and that helps. He can't scream when he's drinking gasoline and after drinking so much he thinks if he screams his stomach will come flying up through his mouth and it will fly away until it reaches the sky and then it too will be eaten by whatever evil waits out there.

If he remembered what death was, Rambo would have wished for it.

16

Commando thinks he has Rambo just about fixed up. He decides to weld Cobra's face to his stomach, knowing they were always close and this was probably what Cobra would have wanted. Besides, he doesn't think he can eat Cobra's face. He had a bad acne problem and that unibrow. He drains some of his blood into a goblet, mixes it with Gatorade, and manages to choke it down.

The vision he had, the vision the antenna gave him, was of two robots. He originally thought those were supposed to be Rambo and Cobra but Cobra was dead, which left only him. It's a drastic decision and he finds himself hesitant. He thinks about God's Mountaineers. Maybe he needs to leave the scrap yard. Maybe he needs to go check things out. If he gets into town and every beautiful girl is there with Gravedigger John and they're all huddled around a mountain of corpses, holding hands and singing hymns to God, maybe he'll think about it.

He dips a siphon hose into one of the tanks of gasoline and puts the other end in Rambo's mouth, tells him he'll be back.

Rambo's eyes are rolled back in his head.

Commando tells him to wait for the voice. He tells him it comes from space. He tells him it speaks the knowledge. He tells him it's called intuitive knowledge and knows Rambo doesn't know what the hell that means.

He hops in the El Camino and drives into town, the sun low in the sky.

17

Commando can see the mountain of corpses at least a mile out of town. By the time he reaches it, he's nearly seasick. He has the windows down and the smell is atrocious. He visited a slaughterhouse one time and that smell was similar. But this was much worse. Death and rot. He parks the car in the parking lot of a shop, amidst other junked and burned-out cars. He wonders who did all this destruction if there isn't anyone left.

He wants to see what God's Mountaineers are doing but he doesn't want them to see him. He's afraid they'll drag him in, turn him into one of them. He's afraid that's what he wants.

On the other hand, it could be a trap. Gravedigger John was never the most trustworthy fellow. It's possible he just wanted to lure them into town so he could use them for food or something even worse. But he'd had his chance with Rambo and Cobra if that was the case.

Commando opens the door of an antique store, goes to the back room, and finds a ladder to the roof. He can't believe the Mountaineers are building a mountain of corpses just to honor God or the dead or whatever. He thinks the voice they're hearing is similar to the one he has heard. There has to be something else behind it. Maybe the mountain is going to come alive and be a mass of dead humans. He read a story where something like that happened. Things have changed and he wouldn't say anything was impossible. Early on, when he had watched the news reports, he saw evidence of it. He never questioned it because it was on television before the television went to a test pattern and then to static and then just black.

It was from the first day of the rain. Footage from Central Park in New York. There were three things he saw. The first was a man with an eagle's head. The second was a person standing with his arms outstretched, Christ-like, with a smaller person crawling out of his mouth and then drifting into a panicked crowd. The third was a man dressed in a suit walking into and disappearing into a tree. This was all amidst a lot of chaos and screaming and sheets of slags raining down from the trash galaxy, but these were the things he focused on and he thought maybe he was the only person who saw them and then, weeks later, when he was still alive, he thought maybe this meant something. Maybe he was chosen.

He stands on the roof and looks at the mountain of corpses. It is the most depressing thing he has ever seen. Most of them are not whole. Most of them are hollowed out shells, the slags eating away their insides while their skins hang in rotten gray folds. Black blood runs down the mountain slowly and collects in the gutter. And there, at the foot of the mountain, he sees God's Mountaineers. There are quite a few of them. Maybe a hundred. There would have to be to be able to move that amount of corpses in such a short period of time.

About ten of them play an odd assortment of instruments and not very well. Some of them are singing. Some of them are dancing that blissed out hippie dance Commando has seen on footage of Woodstock and every bad concert he's ever been to. Some of them are writhing on the ground, in the blood, smearing it over their bodies, over their faces, onto their lips.

Men.

Women.

Children.

Commando has never felt so alone.

This will not save them.

The voice is loud and clear. Coming through the antenna, radiating down through every bone in his skeleton.

This will not save them.

The god they're praying to is dead and they're too optimistic to see that.

And it becomes clear what he has to do.

Protect them.

Yes.

Commando feels something he's never really felt before kick up inside him, some synchronous harmony moving him along, back downstairs, back down to the car, back to the scrap yard.

18

Rambo can't struggle anymore. He lies there and looks up at the black sea, imagines unicorns swimming in it, thrashing wildly around, possibly drowning, before glowing dots float to the surface, jellyfish intended to snare the unicorns, and then his mind goes blank. He feels a hum begin at the top of his skull and spread down through his body and he's filled with something like cool contentment.

19

Commando reaches the scrap yard after dark. He feels renewed and purposeful. It is no longer as difficult to eat the flesh of Cobra. Throughout the night, he gorges himself. Rambo has stopped thrashing and moaning but he seems to be alive. His metal chest rises and falls. He touches his scythe antenna and feels it vibrating with the same energy surging through *his* body. Rambo needs nourishment and he feeds him the raw flesh of Cobra as well, filling his body with both essential toxins and nutrients. He unties Rambo and he doesn't fight back or attempt to run away.

The next morning Commando begins transforming himself and making alterations to Rambo. He gives him a hammer for a right hand and a wrench for the left. He gives himself a hook for a hand. Time gets weird. It feels like it stretches out. Commando and Rambo wander around the scrap yard, drinking gasoline and stripping Cobra's flesh from his bone. Commando searches through the washing machines and finds that most of them still have clothes in them. Like the antennas, this is another mystery. Another something he's never noticed before. He guesses there are a lot of things he's never noticed before and wonders how many of those things are really important.

He begins opening the trunks of the cars until he finds two pairs of shoes large enough to fit their new robot bodies.

He thought he would feel pain with all this metal bolted into his flesh. But he doesn't feel pain. He feels calm. He feels and knows he is waiting for something. He feels some sense of strange communion with Rambo he's never felt before, even though neither of them say a word.

And he feels powerful. Almost indestructible.

20

Commando and Rambo are drinking oil out of metal goblets when the tornado sirens sound. Before the slags, they set them off at noon on the first Monday of every month and it was something Commando never got used to. He knew they were tornado sirens and he knew they were just testing them, but they made him think of nuclear war, just like the emergency broadcast tests always made him think of zombie invasions. He hasn't heard the sirens since the first storm of slags.

Commando unscrews Rambo's antenna and pours one jug of gasoline and one jug of piss down the hole. Rambo does the same for him.

They begin their walk to town.

They move quickly, their heavy feet crunching down the middle of the road.

The corpse mountain is even larger than it was the first time Commando saw it. The corpses extend at least four stories into the air, line the sides of the streets. Neither Commando nor Rambo sees anyone else. Commando imagines them hiding amidst the corpses in the mountain. Or they've built something like a hut at the center of the mountain, thinking that by surrounding themselves with death, they could keep themselves from it. Someone has lit all the buildings on fire. Once he didn't need his right hand anymore, Commando fastened a tube to it and stuffed it with rags. He touches the rags to the fire and lifts them to his head. He feels the fire quickly surge through his body. He does the same to Rambo. Together they begin ascending the mountain of corpses. Their instrument hands provide perfect traction against the sick gore-slicked surfaces of the decaying bodies.

When they reach the top they look to the horizon and see, against the gray sky, a dust cloud barreling toward them.

Commando thinks it could be filled with slags or could be filled with salvation.

The flames hollow him out and he feels himself melt into the metal he has encased himself with.

He hears the voice saying, "Protect," and prepares to fight.

21

Rambo looks at Commando, his head spouting flames, and feels alive and aware for the first time in a really long time. He can feel the slags that have eaten up his brain and the insides of his body crackling and burning. He can hear the dust cloud on the horizon whirling around itself, the grains of dirt and debris frictioning off each other. And somewhere, possibly below him, possibly buried in the center of the corpse mountain, he thinks he hears singing.

PART FOUR

ALL ALONE
AT THE
EDGE OF THE WORLD

1

Darren Welch named his lighter "Luke."

He flicks the small maggot-like thing crawling up his arm onto the floor and collapses onto his knees, bending over it. The little thing is called a "slag." He thinks it describes them pretty well. Little slug-like maggots or maggot-like slugs. Slags. The scientific community didn't stick around long enough to give them a more proper name. It doesn't matter much now anyway.

Luke is a black Bic and Darren cringes at the thought of him running out of fluid and dying. Dying like everyone else.

Hunkering down over the slag, upside down and wriggling on the plank wood floor of the beach house, he sparks the lighter and touches it to the small thing. Its slimy hide blackens and he imagines its insides boiling before exploding through the casing with that weird sick stench he has become accustomed to. A cross between burnt beans and sewage. Texture-wise, he tries to think of it as a sausage. It's even worse that he has to eat the fuckers to stay alive. Imagine that, he thinks, these things have consumed virtually everyone on the planet and now he is here, all alone at what feels like the edge of the world, eating them so he doesn't die from starvation.

Quickly, without thinking about it, he grabs it between two fingers and pops it into his mouth, aiming for the back of his tongue so he doesn't have to taste it. He chokes it down and stands up. He crosses the living room of the house and pulls a cigarette from the mantel. The room is bare. He has used all the furniture as firewood. Soon, he will have to start pulling the floorboards from the upstairs and using them as kindling. He puts the cigarette between his lips and flicks Luke again.

Killing the slags and lighting cigarettes are the things Luke is best at. These are just about the only things Darren has to do. Luke makes him feel like he has an accomplice. He smokes a lot. Smokes and thinks about the way things were.

He thinks about the way things were before and he thinks about the tent down the beach and he holds Luke in his hand, rubbing his thumb up and down the smooth plastic case.

2

One day, life had been normal. The next day the slags had come and changed everything. Were they airborne? he wonders. He remembers them raining from the sky before scurrying after the people—into homes, into businesses, into schools—everywhere. Theories of war were immediately hatched. Terrorists, the Americans said. Others probably said the slags were a distinctly Western invention, typical of American pomposity and aggression. It only took a few days for absolutely none of that to matter. From what Darren can figure, the slags managed to burrow under one's skin or enter through various orifices and release some kind of digestive poison, reducing one's insides to a gray jelly-ish substance. The slags consumed this substance with glee.

Before the plague, Darren had had a wife and children back in Indiana. The children went first and Darren didn't like to think about them because thinking about them made him sad. He knows he will never see them again unless heaven isn't the lie he believes it to be. Thankfully, he didn't have to watch them die, to be consumed by those hideous things. He had just checked on the two boys, playing in their room, when the storm hit. Darren had looked outside and then said to Lora, his wife, "That's some *weeeird* fuckin' rain," thinking nothing more of it. When he went to get the boys for lunch, they were two piles of bones sitting in the midst of their toys and the room was acrawl with the slags. That quickly.

Lora hadn't lasted much longer. Opening the boys' door had released them through the house. They were upon him and he rapidly wiped them off. Returning to the living room, he saw them on Lora and then *in* Lora. Darren remembered her leaning over the kitchen sink a little later, vomiting up blood and he had put his hand on her back, as he always did when she was sick, and he could feel those things *wriggling* beneath the fabric of her shirt. And then she, too, was gone. Loose skin hanging over bones and then those things collapsing her eyes and crawling from the sockets, making holes from the inside of her skin so they could get out and move on.

He hadn't known why he had been spared. He was not immune to the burrowing of the slags although they did not seem to cover him with the profusion they covered others. Still, his body was covered with scars where he had to cut inside his skin and dig them out so they didn't chance upon a major artery. He *is* apparently immune to their poison or saliva or whatever the hell it is that wastes one's insides. He traveled from the quiet Indiana suburb to what he is pretty sure is Maryland before finding this house on the beach and deciding he had run out of land and, really, what was the point of pressing onward? He hasn't seen another single soul on his journey.

Not after the second wave. The one that got his family.

The first wave was bad enough but it resulted in little more than quarantines in all the major cities and, over a several month stretch, infiltration into the mid-size cities and even smaller towns. But it was manageable. It seemed, after a while, that the humans were even winning, beating back the slags.

And then the second wave hit and destroyed all optimism within only a couple of days.

The slags had consumed the food after consuming the population. There isn't anything left. Darren is lonely and terrified. Terrified because the slags are getting bigger. Soon, he will have to fear being mauled more than he will have to fear being poisoned. Humans, he knows, are not immune to mauling.

3

About a half mile down the flat, rough beach stands a red and white tent. He has always wanted to walk to the tent but he has found himself reluctant to give up on life. He reckons he should have gone when the slags were smaller and more harmless. Now he doesn't think he will be able to get more than a tenth the distance without being taken down. He is pretty sure the slags are so hungry they are eating themselves. The good news is, with the size increase, there is an overall population decrease.

He stands at the north window of the house and looks toward the tent. He imagines it filled with happy people. Summer people. He imagines friends and laughter, plans hatched in youth, a whole world waiting. Anything but the waste strewn out behind him.

Today is the day, he tells himself. The longer he waits, the bigger and more threatening the slags will become. While the ones that make it into the house are still on the small side, the ones on the outside now resemble something that makes him think of kickballs and melons. Next week it will probably be giant pumpkins. The week after that, he will have to stop thinking about fruits and vegetables and start using adjectives—dwarfish, average, giant . . .

Yes. If he is going to the tent, it has to be soon. He doesn't even really know why going to the tent is important. Maybe because it is the only thing besides this house breaking up the monotony of the beach. Without the tent, it would just be sand and ocean, sand and ocean—as far as the eye could see.

He lights another cigarette, not even remembering tossing the previous one out, and turns his attention back to the desolate gray beach. A dirty white bird swoops down toward the coarse sand. Birds are the only signs of any life besides the slags he has seen. Even as the bird swoops down, he thinks, *No, you don't want to do that.* But the stupid thing touches down on the beach and a bloated slag rises from the sand, taking the bird down with surprising dexterity. The bird becomes immediately limp, the slag's mouth clamped down over its neck, not a drop of blood escaping. Soon, two other slags scramble out of the sand nearby and scuttle toward their meal.

He thinks it best to move while at least some of them are distracted. He knows he will have to run just about the entire distance. He drops his cigarette to the floor and stamps on it, flicking one of the baby slags from his skin, grabbing the pistol housing a single bullet and flinging himself through the door, being careful to shut it against the creatures so he will have a place to come back to.

He runs as fast as he can along the beach thinking the tent must be absolutely filled with slags. It's probably like their home or something. And he is running toward it. No. It can't be their home. He knows he doesn't really believe that. If that were the case then what would the point of running to it be? He isn't sure he attaches any type of divine significance to his being what may very well be the last person on earth but he wants to continue living enough to want to believe there is something in that tent.

Midway there, he decides maybe the tent is a doorway to some other world. A world without the slags. A world just like the one he has come from because, despite his disagreements with that world, he has found himself, more and more, thinking of it as a place of near perfection. And however fucked up it was, it seemed that humans had been the cause of most of the really major fuck-ups. But they seemed able to recover from their fuck-ups. Then the slags came. Darren would take the humans back in a heartbeat.

He continues to run, fighting the sand, pressing onward. The sand fills his running shoes. He hates that feeling. Wishes he had just left his shoes off completely.

Yes, he tells himself, the tent is a doorway to another world and those people he has imagined in there . . . They are people from that world. They came to the tent to have parties and wait for him. Maybe they were transported there. He can practically hear their soft laughter and smell their exotic food.

His foot hits something hard and he goes shooting forward, knocked off his feet. He scrambles to his knees before one of the slags plows into his chest, driving him down into the sand. The tiny particles invade his nose and eyes and he can hear and feel the thing's teeth puncture his leg.

He cries out in pain, looks down at the thing. Twisting around, he casts his glance back toward the tent. More slags, larger slags, come from that direction.

He doesn't think he is going to make it to the tent today.

Standing up, he knows he should remove the thing from his leg. But that will take too much time. A paranoid part of him says maybe these larger ones also contain a more toxic venom he isn't immune to. He dismisses that notion, figuring having his insides liquefied is better than standing here and being mauled by this slag's cousin. He will drag it back to the house with him and then he will show it why it shouldn't have fucked with him. The running is a little slower and he is accosted by two more slags. Swinging out the leg that already has the slag attached, he fends them off. They tumble away and begin fighting amongst themselves. If only he could turn all of them against each other.

4

Finally, he reaches the house, practically throwing himself inside. He is weak with blood loss and pain. The blood, at least, he will be getting back at dinner.

Holding the gun by the barrel, he bashes at the slag's head and mouth, not really caring that he occasionally slips and bashes himself in the shin. The most important thing is separating himself from this parasite. Once it releases its grip on his leg, Darren pulls Luke from his pocket, flicks it past a couple of sparks until there is flame and then holds the flame to the two gaping holes on his leg, cauterizing them. He clenches his teeth together and grunts, spewing forth every curse he knows.

He looks at the slag on the floor and knows he will have a feast tonight. Maybe it will be the highlight to an otherwise disappointing day. Until he remembers the taste. He can't imagine that taste magnified to the size of this thing. He almost thinks he would prefer to eat a steaming pile of his own shit.

Eventually, he does eat the giant slag. He eats little bites at a time. They are heinous and he thinks he would rather be dead. Still, long after the thing has rotted, he continues to eat. Luke chars little bite-size pieces, dulling the taste.

Luke gets sick, spitting out little sparks before producing a low flame. Darren is sure to use Luke's dying breaths to get a nice fire started in the fireplace. He has been lazy about this the past few days. One day, Luke stops producing a flame. Darren figures that is pretty much the death of the lighter. He puts him in the pocket of his stinking jeans. Occasionally, he pulls him out and flicks him, hoping he will kick out a flame, however small.

5

More and more, Darren holds the gun. It's a hefty little Glock that isn't really so little. Darren names the gun "Gary." Gary the Glock, he thinks it has a nice ring to it.

Will he ever use it?

He doesn't know. He's left one bullet in there for a reason but he continues to hold on to some dying hope.

The slags continue to grow until they become giants. Some of them are nearly as tall as the house and Darren figures any chance he has of escape is over. Even worse, they seem to know he is in the house. They circle hungrily, pressing their sick little snouts to the windows and sniffing. Jesus, he thinks, if you're going to take me just come in and do it.

He sleeps more and more. Every day seems gray. The ocean is an endless rhythm, lulling him to sleep. He has lost so much weight he can encircle his biceps with his hand.

One morning, he's awakened by the house shaking. He doesn't know what is going on. He doesn't really want to know what is going on but figures it out anyway. The slags are lifting the house from its moorings. At first, he wants to believe they are taking him to the tent. The house and the tent, what a lovely romance, he thinks. But he isn't going toward the tent. He's going toward the ocean. They march him out and release the house. Careful to make sure he still has Gary, Darren scrabbles up to the attic, out the window and onto the roof.

It's kind of like a boat. He is a captain, going out to sea. No. It is more like a Viking funeral and he thinks about touching Luke to the shingles to see if they will burst into flame until he remembers Luke is dead.

The lapping waves drag him directionally toward the tent but further out to sea. He looks longingly at the opening of the tent. Yes. He is sure he can see fabulous things inside. At this very moment, he is sure he sees a woman, a beautiful woman with long blond hair, pass through the flaps and stare out at the violent sun bursting over the ocean.

Darren looks at Gary. Sinister Gary. Blessed Gary. Gary with his promises to make all of this go away. Then he looks at the tent.

He dives into the ocean and swims.

6

He tries to keep the figure on the beach in focus but the waves are choppy and he's swimming more or less one-handed, trying to keep Gary above the water. He doesn't think Gary will like water much at all. He desperately plunges his legs into the water, trying to find purchase but he just goes under, sucking the salty water into his mouth. He rises above the water and coughs.

The beach comes back into view. He must be about fifty feet out. If the figure is still there, he can't see her. It's possible she's covered up by the slags standing on the beach. There are at least ten of them.

Shit.

Darren figures he has two choices. He can either give up where he is and let the sea reclaim him, take him for good. Or he can reach the beach and use the one bullet he has left to shoot himself in the head. Provided Gary will even shoot. The waves take him under again and he bobs to the surface and vomits out the ocean water.

He rolls over onto his back and relaxes. There isn't really any reason to be in a hurry to reach the beach since it will most likely mean death. Lying on his back and looking up at the blue sky is more relaxing and it feels more productive. With each tug of the waves, he goes shooting toward shore. He looks at his house out in the ocean. He figures there must be slags out here too. They're everywhere. He's known that for a very long time. He feels stupid for getting his hopes up.

He tries to stand again and this time, his feet find the rough sand. He turns around and walks toward the beach. Even from here, he can tell the slags are twice as tall as he is. They even have fully formed arms and legs, although they are much thinner than their bodies. Now they are neither slug- nor maggot-like. They are, if anything, more human-like.

He presses Gary to his temple and walks slowly toward the waiting line of slags.

Darren hears a loud sound and he jumps and accidentally squeezes the trigger.

7

Click.

His body goes immediately slack with . . . is it relief or fear? Didn't he *want* the gun to go off? Didn't he want the gun to scatter his brains all over the beach so he didn't have to face indubitable mauling from the slags?

No.

Because he heard that other shot and once he recovers from nearly wasting himself, he realizes the slag in the middle is missing its head. It staggers out to him, a couple wobbly steps on its too thin legs before plunging into the sand on the beach, some kind of yellow-tinged liquid running from where its neck would be if it were human.

Then there's another shot and another slag's head erupts.

And another.

And another.

And Darren knows there's no point in standing around and waiting for things to get better than this. He digs his feet into the sand and takes off running toward the tent hoping whoever is doing the shooting will cover him if one of the few remaining slags makes a lunge at him.

Running to the right of the slags, they shift and try to run toward him. They were probably quicker as crawlers. Their running is shaky and not very fast.

Another one erupts and then another one and Darren is almost to the tent. He keeps his eyes focused on it. The shooter must be hiding just behind the flap of the tent.

The final slag drops to its knees, crouches down, and springs toward him like a snake. He throws himself into the sand, thinking maybe he can crawl the rest of the way. There's another shot and he knows that slag is dead, as well. He reaches the tent and stands up.

He realizes his beautiful woman is not beautiful at all. She might not even be a woman. She is very large.

"Follow me!" she barks over her shoulder and Darren does.

She is charging toward a fire blazing in the middle of the tent. She looks like a football player in a summer dress. She dives into the fire and Darren swears her hair separates from her head but he doesn't give himself time to think about it and dives in after her.

8

The flames engulf him and he thinks maybe he has just done a very stupid thing. But he figures the end result is going to be the same, given his choices. He just wouldn't have chosen to be burned alive.

But the flames are only momentary and then he's falling through blackness before landing in ice cold water. For a moment it feels like he loses consciousness and then he feels hands wrapping around his arms and pulling him out of the water. He opens his eyes but everything is a black and orange flickering swirl. He's standing on his feet and rubbing his eyes and looking around and trying to make sense of it all. He vomits out some water. He's surrounded by the smell of burning hair and people. Faces. People like him.

He sees the woman he followed into the flames. She isn't really a woman at all. A man with a large hairy mole on his left cheek. He's holding the charred wig in his hands, wringing it out. To his left is an extremely thin man with an eyepatch. He's wearing one of those black military sweaters, the kind with the leather patch on the shoulder. To his left stands a woman who might have been attractive at one time. There are more people behind them. People who are moving closer to the commotion, trying to see who has joined them. The room is long and narrow and cave-like, lit by torches.

The man with the eyepatch takes a step toward Darren.

He thrusts out a bony hand.

"My name's Mark Shell," he says. "I'm the leader here."

"Where . . ." Darren stammers. "Where is here?"

"Underground."

Darren continues looking around. They have to be pretty deep under the ground. It doesn't seem possible. The tent wasn't more than twenty feet away from the ocean at high tide. If they were this far underground they should be covered in water and wet sand. Buried.

"How?" Darren says. If he can clear away just a little bit of the confusion, he can start making some sense of everything.

"How?" Shell asks, almost mockingly.

"How are we underground? There should be water."

"Let me introduce Pearl." Shell motions to the maybe attractive girl to his left. "She's the queen of a town called Hollow City. Or, she used to be. She's able to make things happen. She's a good person to have on our side. Come on," Shell approaches Darren and throws an arm around him. "You need some food and some rest."

And he drags him back into the underground lair and he's fed better food than he has had in a very long time.

<h1 style="text-align:center">9</h1>

While eating, Darren can't help observing the people around him. They are all dressed as Shell is. Even the man who had been dressed like a woman is now wearing the black paramilitary gear. Except they all have one sleeve that extends to the very end of their hands, so it looks like they have one hand and one extra long arm. They all move about rapidly and look very busy. They speak quickly in clipped tones, as though there isn't any time for lazy conversation.

Darren notices a lot of slags.

Some of them hang on the walls, in various states of evisceration. Some of them move about freely. Some of them are alive and chained throughout the lair. Some of them are tiny. Some of them are as large as he is.

He finishes eating his spaghetti in a can, moves the can aside and leans forward onto the table, resting his head on his arms. It feels nice. He feels safe here, even with all the slags. Maybe it's all the humans. Maybe it's all the paramilitary gear.

Shell sits down on the bench across the table from him and raps on the wood.

"Listen here," he says. "There are some things I should tell you about our operation but first I need to ask you if you mind losing your left arm."

"Losing my left arm?"

"Yeah. Like having it lopped off."

"Yes. I would have to say that I am opposed to losing my left arm."

"Then you can't be part of us."

"What? Because I don't want you to lop off my arm? That's crazy."

"Nobody said it wasn't crazy. Of course it's crazy. Everything here is crazy. But it's the way it has to be. Are you in or are you out?"

"Is there a reason why?"

"Are you in or are you out?"

Darren thinks about it. He looks around at all the scurrying personnel. They have all apparently had their left arms lopped off. But something fills out their sweaters. Do they have prostheses? He doesn't really want to have his arm lopped off—either the right or the left. But what is the alternative? Go back to the surface and let the slags devour him?

"So you would really feed me to the slags if I don't agree to let you lop off my arm?"

"We'd have no choice."

Darren shakes his head in wonderment. These seem to be the only people left in the world and they are out of their fucking heads. Great.

"It doesn't seem very safe."

"Yes or no?"

"Yes. Okay. You can take my left arm."

He has no idea why he is agreeing to this but doesn't really see any alternative. He could try and kill this man with the one sparkling crazy eye sitting across from him, he guesses. He could kill him and then convince everyone he's crazy and they don't really need to sacrifice their arms. But he doesn't think that will work either. Leaders can't be replaced that easily and he doesn't really think he's leadership material anyway. Besides, what would be the point? They'd already lost *their* arms.

"Very good," Shell says and stands up from the table. "Follow me."

He follows Shell toward the back of the lair. A few people stop what they are doing to look at Darren. He can't figure if it's pity or hunger in their eyes.

"Pearl!" Shell calls. "We need to begin the procedure."

As Pearl joins Shell, Darren continues to follow them. He is struck with a sense of vertigo. It doesn't feel like anything in this lair is solid. It's all wet sand trying to fill in the hole that is the lair. That's why everyone seems so frenetic. They are working to continuously push back the walls. But what for? Why here? There have to be a million other hiding places. He follows Shell and Pearl through a door but it isn't really a door at all. More like a waterfall of sand, just enough to occlude what happens behind it.

"There's absolutely nothing to worry about," Shell says over his shoulder.

Darren looks around the claustrophobic room they've just entered. A flattened mound of sand that makes him immediately think of a hospital bed or a mortuary slab. A sword submerged in a barrel of fire. A slag dangling from a rope in the sandy ceiling. Darren wonders what is keeping the rope in there and thinks he probably has a whole lot to worry about.

10

Hesitant, Darren stands at the opening of the room.

"Come on," Shell says. "It's just an arm. Stop being such a fucking candyass."

Just an arm, Darren thinks. Then, first noticing it as she withdraws the sword from the barrel, Darren points to Pearl and says, "Why does *she* still have her left arm?"

"Because she's the Queen of Town. We wouldn't be here if it weren't for her."

"Maybe *you* wouldn't be here."

"Look, we don't have all day. You wanna do it while the sword is still sterile or you wanna wait until it's crawling with bacteria?"

Darren looks at the glowing sword.

"We find it works best if you're lying down."

Darren slumps his shoulders and approaches the weird sand

table. He hops up onto it and lies back, staring at the brown ceiling. Shell tosses him a hank of cloth and says, "Bite down on that."

Darren thinks taking advice from one who has already lost his left arm is a good idea. He bites down on the musty tasting cloth. Shell grabs his left arm and pulls it out straight. Pearl stands about where Darren's knees are, raises the sword above her head and brings it down. Darren hears it cutting the air and feels a sharp and savage heat attack his shoulder before blacking out.

11

He comes to, bleary-eyed. After peeling his eyes open and rubbing them with his right fist, he looks over at his left arm. He sees a pus-colored mass, roughly the same size and shape as his arm. There is a bit of pain at his shoulder but it doesn't hurt nearly as much as he thought it would. Beyond the shoulder, he can't feel anything. Is this his new arm? Why cut it off if they were just going to replace it with another, inferior arm?

He pokes his new left arm and it twitches. The end of it, where his hand used to be, bends toward him and . . . snaps at him. There's an opening there. It looks like a toothed anus.

Fuck! They replaced his arm with a slag!

What the hell kind of nightmare is this?

He screams out with the business end of the slag snapping just a couple inches in front of his face.

"What are you waiting for?" Shell says from the foot of the bed. "You have to show it who's in control."

"You cut off my arm and put a fucking slag in its place?!" Darren squeals. He doesn't like the sound of his voice. He sounds weak and hysterical.

Shell chuckles. "We most certainly did."

"Are you fucking insane? Why the fuck would you do that?" He's still squealing.

"Who knows? It was Pearl's idea."

"Yet she's the only one without a . . . slag arm."

"A slarm."

"That's fucking precious."

"It's good to see you have a bit of your old spirit back."

The slarm continues trying to chomp at his face. He waits until the anus mouth closes and slams his fist into it.

"There," Shell says. "See. It's not all that hard. They can learn. Make something a part of you and, before long, it begins thinking it is."

Darren slings his legs off the bed and pulls himself into a sitting position. He feels woozy. "There has to be a reason for this." He says this and realizes he's thinking out loud. He doesn't specifically mean the slag flesh-welded to his shoulder. He means everything. There has to be a reason he survived the second attack. There has to be a reason he stayed alive in the beach house. There has to be a reason why he is here now.

"You'll learn more about it at training," Shell says, presumably meaning the arm but, at this point, Darren wouldn't really be surprised if he means everything as well.

"Training?"

"Yes, training. But you're here pretty late in the game so you'll have two sessions, at most. But that's okay. They're pretty fast learners."

"What are you training for?"

"The attack, of course. The reverse apocalypse."

"The reverse apocalypse?"

"Yes. We're taking the world back from the slags."

"How do you plan on doing that? There can't be more than twenty people out there."

"Twenty *well-trained* people. And Pearl. You can't forget Pearl. She's worth . . . well, a whole lot more than just one person."

"Do you worship her or something? I think you should put your faith in more realistic things."

"I've seen exactly what Pearl can do." Shell moves closer to Darren until their faces are almost touching. "She once hid herself in my eye socket for hours. She started small. Then she got bigger and had to come out. She filled me up and then emptied me out, sewed up the husk with a piece of my rib and strands of her hair. Then she breathed my soul back into my body. Does that sound like just anyone to you? Have you ever done that?"

This only convinces Darren that Shell is completely insane.

"I guess we'll just have to wait and see."

"After all, it's not like we don't have a plan."

"And what is this plan?"

"We're going to Hollow City by way of fugue. Hollow City was one of the safe zones after the first wave. They have the highest concentration of immune anywhere in this area."

"Isn't that in Ohio?"

"Yes."

"And we're in Maryland. How's that 'in the area'?"

"Connected by fugue."

"Ah. Connected by fugue. Makes perfect sense. That's good, I guess. Very sound reasoning."

"Talking to you is like shitting and then playing with it. Training's in one hour."

Shell rushes from the room, leaving Darren to sit there and shake his head and wish he had been mercilessly devoured by slags on the shore.

12

He continues sitting there because he doesn't know what else to do. He guesses he could go out and mingle with the rest of the people down here but they had all seemed pretty preoccupied and frantic. He knows he doesn't want to go out there and push sand around for the next hour. Maybe he's too lazy or maybe he just isn't a team player. He tells himself it's because he needs time to adjust to his new arm.

Maybe he nods off but it seems like the hour passes very quickly. When he comes to it's to the sound of Shell shouting at him from the entranceway.

"Come on! Come on! Come on! You're gonna be late."

Darren slides down off the slab and, as he passes Shell, says, "You know, I don't really have to do anything you tell me to do. I'm here of my own free will."

Shell jerks his slarm toward the drippy ceiling and says, "You could just as easily be back up there of *my* own free will. Now move your ass!" And he shakes the end of his slarm in front of Darren's face where it gnashes its teeth. Shell is very persuasive, Darren thinks. He follows the others into another chamber. Shell and Pearl do not enter.

Entering the chamber, Darren counts the other troops. Eighteen. Eighteen plus himself and Shell and Pearl and they are going to wage war on a town of slags. It doesn't seem like a very good idea.

In the chamber with them are at least an equal number of slags. He guesses this is the training. They are not full-grown slags. These days, full grown slags are probably as large as most houses. These are slightly larger than the ones comprising their slarms.

The other troops look crazed but methodical. They waste no time approaching the slags. Darren stands back and observes for a few seconds. With the left arm being replaced by a slag, he has no immediate desire to lose his right one. He watches a frail woman with a shock of dirty brown hair bare her teeth as she stands two feet in front of a slag. The slag coils up and throws itself at her. She shields herself using her slarm. The slag latches onto it. The woman reaches toward her belt and pulls up a large knife. She begins hacking at the slag hungrily clamped to her arm. Eventually it releases its hold and drops thickly to the floor. The woman crouches over it and her slarm takes over. It whips down and quickly plunges into one of the wounds opened by the knife. After a few seconds, the slag on the floor appears thin and lifeless. The woman turns and goes off to hunt another slag.

Toward the back of the chamber, Darren hears a scream. He turns to see a man down on his back, wildly kicking his legs. A slag has its teeth buried into the man's side and his slarm is busy feeding at his eye socket. Darren looks down at his slarm and hopes it does not try to betray him. He decides to test it out by coming to the downed man's aid.

He approaches cautiously, ready to let his slarm clamp onto the slag devouring the man's side but a burly man to his left knocks his slarm away.

"No." The man shakes his head as if cautioning him.

"But he's being devoured."

"Then so it is. We must divide the strong from the weak."

"I'm more about safety in numbers," Darren says and guides his slarm toward the slag. It just hangs there in front, dangling limp and flaccid. Great, he thinks, all the slags in the world and I get the retarded one. He slaps it on the back of the head, nearly throwing it at the slag.

"I can't let you do this." The burly man is walking back toward the entrance of the chamber. "Shell! Shell!"

"Motherfucker," Darren hisses and begins kicking at the slag gnawing on the dead man.

Shell rushes into the chamber and storms over to Darren. He puts a hand on his shoulder and spins him around so he'll stop kicking the slag. Shell sticks his face in front of Darren's and flicks him on the forehead.

"What the hell's the matter with you?" Shell barks.

"I was trying to keep this man from getting eaten."

"Terry said he told you you weren't supposed to do that."

"Terry's a dick."

"You're a dick. And your training's over. You come out until everyone finishes and then you're on clean-up detail."

Darren wants to argue with him but sees the resulting outcome as too stupid to even consider. He slumps his shoulders and leaves the chambers. He looks to his left and makes fleeting eye contact with Pearl. If she wasn't filthy she would be pretty striking, he thinks. Sex is so far behind him he doesn't even think about it. He just puts his head down and wanders around, realizing he doesn't have anywhere to wander to.

13

Clean-up isn't the chore Shell had undoubtedly intended it to be. Darren had cleaned up and eaten countless slags. They had little to no effect on him when they were dead. He uses the shovel and wheelbarrow provided and wheels the remains out into the main chamber. The others are gathered around a long table and Darren realizes he is probably wheeling out their dinner. He had hoped they had something more exotic to eat down here. He should have known. They'd gotten his hopes up with the canned food. So far this place hasn't really shown him any perks of living with other people. Darren lets the wheelbarrow rest next to Shell, standing at the head of the table.

Beside Shell is a rusted metal barrel with a grill grate over the top and flames guttering down below. At least they are going to cook the slags before eating them. There is an open spot at the very end of the table. Darren walks down there and sits. No one speaks. They stare reverently toward the head of the table, toward Shell and Pearl. Darren wonders how long everyone has been here. He wonders if they have been brainwashed somehow. Or maybe they're just desperate. He wonders if Shell and Pearl actually have a plan or if it's just some dream they hold over everyone's head. If it *is* a dream. It sounds more like a nightmare to Darren.

Dinner is consumed in silence. Darren's slag is undercooked. Many people gag while eating the slag meat. Darren takes that to mean they are still moderately human. He wants to ask them if they know they are going to their deaths. Do they realize what the slags have become? Do they really think there are other people out there?

That night he gets to sleep and actually feels a modicum of safety for the first time since the attacks. They sleep in two-hour shifts because if they all slept at once they would end up buried.

The next training session goes much more smoothly. Darren doesn't try to help anyone. Luckily, the only person who was in danger of being consumed was the frail looking woman from the day before. The slag she was battling had clamped itself onto her slarm and she had, in turn, devoured the attacking slag like a wild animal.

That night, at dinner, Shell announces: "Rest up tonight! Tomorrow the fugue will arrive and we will take it to Hollow City!"

The troops look down at the blackened slag meat on their plates. They do not seem very excited. After dinner, they break up to go about pushing the walls of the chamber back. Darren finds Shell milling around and approaches him.

"I need to talk to you," Darren says.

Shell turns his head and says, "Speak."

"I just wanted to find out if you're really serious about this. When was the last time you were above ground for any period of time?"

"Let me stop you right there, trooper. I've heard it all before. And it's not like that. It's not a matter of being outnumbered. I know what the slags have become. They've become giants. They've become so much more than they were. But they can't win because we're the chosen."

"Chosen by whom?"

Shell shakes his head. "You don't understand anything, do you?"

"I guess not," Darren says. "Maybe you could explain."

"You can't explain faith. Do you know what faith is? Having faith in something is to believe in it unconditionally. Pearl is the chosen. She's like Jesus or something. I've explained to you a little about what she can do and you'll get to see her do a lot more tomorrow. Maybe then you'll understand. Can you do me that favor? Can you put off your doubts until tomorrow? What are the alternatives, really? It doesn't seem like so much to ask. You can go above ground and die, live out your remaining days alone and in fear, or you can actually believe in something. I think you'll find it feels pretty good to believe in something."

Darren doesn't want to agree with him but he doesn't necessarily want to argue either. He walks away silently, figuring that's a happy medium.

He isn't able to sleep that night.

14

Bleary-eyed, he watches the flurry of activity around him. The troops, led by Pearl and Shell, march toward the pool beneath the ring of fire. Pearl hoists up her skirt and climbs into the pool. The skirt floats up around her.

"Everybody in! Everybody in!" Shell shouts.

Darren thinks this is the stupidest thing in the world. He's the last one in the pool, except for Shell. Everyone is gathered around Pearl. She raises her arms up to the dripping ceiling. The hole has long since closed. He's tempted to reach beneath her skirt and then he sees that everyone is doing exactly that. Even Shell. Especially Shell. His eye is rolled back in his head, his body vibrating with something that could very well be ecstasy. *Dirty old perv,* Darren thinks. But now is not the time to start bucking any trends so he reaches under her skirt as well. It's basically just a mass of other hands at this point. He honestly thought the fugue would be something other than group frottage but, nevertheless, here it was in all its unwashed glory.

And then something does begin happening.

The pool is swirling around them and rising toward the ceiling. It begins going faster and faster, water droplets pelting Darren in the face. He can't see anything. At first the drops sting and then they separate even further until they are a swirling mist. Now he's in some sort of cluster with all the other troops. They've all locked arms around each other and bunched toward the middle, tightening up around Pearl. He thinks he hears her moaning. It could be pleasure or could be the fact that all her bones are being smashed.

Then they are floating en masse and Darren loses all sense of the cavern around him. He loses all sense of the bodies around him. It feels like he's floating through the air. Then he sees Pearl. It's him and Pearl, floating in a cool gray mist over the blighted world. She's moving against him and smiling and she's putting his hands under her dress and he can feel his erection. It's the first one he's had probably since the last time he'd had sex with his wife. Her hands reach toward the button on his militia issue pants and there's a part of him that really wants what might happen except for one disconcerting thought. He imagines Pearl floating through all these other spaces with all these people. He imagines her with gross Terry and creepy Shell. He imagines her going down on the skeletal lady. He realizes he doesn't even know the names of most of the people here. He feels even more alone than he did before and he brushes her hand away. Her smile dissolves and he makes eye contact with her. He feels her *reaching* inside of him with eyes that look like a gray sky with bolts of lightning streaking it. She's trying to control him or something. He looks down. Down at the scary distant ground, smoldering and devastated. She grabs his chin and forces him to make eye contact with her.

You have to.

You have to.

You have to.

It's like a whispered chant inside his head. He tries to shove her away but she isn't going anywhere. He puts his hands over his ears, closes his eyes and screams as loud as he can. It's all muffled in the swirling mass of the fugue and he feels her hands all over him and he tries as hard as he can to make his erection go away. He can't shake the feeling that something very bad is going to happen if she succeeds in this.

Time passes and he can't tell if it's going fast or slow or fast and then slow. He can't tell if they have stopped or if they are continuing to float. He can't tell when he is all alone or when she is all over him. He tries to turn his back on her. He feels her hands on him. Her mouth on him. Anything to coax him into hardness and it's her persistence that solidifies his opinion.

And then he feels the solid ground beneath his feet and he's standing there with the other troops, Pearl at the vanguard. Everyone else carries a look of something like paranoid bliss in their eyes and Darren feels dirt scouring at his skin and hears the screeching roar of slags and a world burning down.

They exit the fugue and come upon the devastated exoskeleton of what used to be Hollow City.

15

Emerging from the fugue, Darren has an immediate sense of badness. It's dark from all the smoke in the air. Standing in front of them is an army of mammoth slags, easily two stories high each. Ten troops are immediately devoured. They've walked into something. Shell was a fool for having faith in Pearl. Whatever parlor tricks she could do, no one could get them out of this.

He snaps to attention and sees a giant toothy mouth in front of him. The opening is as big as a pond. The slag is rearing back its blind head. Before he can feel its teeth cut him in half, just as that enormous head begins its descent, Darren leaps forward into the mouth.

He hears the teeth snap shut and feels the slag's head move around him in something that could very well be confusion. Then he's sliding down its gullet and deep into its body. It smells like decaying meat and bile. Darren throws up, adding to the heady scent. Then he feels movement. They're moving toward something even though Darren feels the only something he's probably headed toward is certain death. He wonders how long it will take for the slag's stomach acid to devour him.

The inside is strange and fleshy, covered in something like oozing mucous. No bones anywhere. Nothing to grab onto. It's only a matter of time before he's sucked down into whatever sick bowel this thing has and that will probably be it. He isn't a worm, isn't a parasite, isn't made to live in shit.

He plunges his hand into the gross mucous of the slag's insides. He sets his slarm to work on the wall. The rapid movement jostles him. The slarm is probably so small it feels like little more than a pinprick to the giant slag. But he doesn't need much to make it out. Just a small opening. Then he can run to . . . where? Where will he run to? Where *can* he run to? This is certainly the end. He just watched half the troop devoured in a matter of seconds.

While his slarm works on the flesh of the slag he thinks about what happened.

It had to have been a set-up. But who was setting them up? Pearl or Shell? It had to be one of them. Darren leans toward the one who did not sacrifice her arm to "the cause." Even though he really wants to believe it's Shell because he's such a prick. He supposes it could be both. Maybe they really do have some idea how to end this and just don't want anybody else around when it happens.

His slarm must be hungry because it tears through the slag with amazing verve. Darren sticks his good arm through the hole and feels what might be air on his fingertips. It's hot and grainy, not wet and slimy. He takes that as a good sign. He sticks the slarm out and lets it clamp onto the outside of the slag to get a good grip and then he rips his way out. He pushes his head through, pulls his body through, wipes the clinging mucous from his eyes and slides down the back of the monstrous slag.

It immediately turns to snap at him but its size, while a great asset, is also a great hindrance. Darren darts for the first narrow spot he sees. A tiny access alley between two storefronts. Midway down the alley he stops to catch his breath and marvels at his brief glimpse of this new world.

The slags are reshaping it. It looks like everything was destroyed and the parts used to make bigger structures. Even the buildings to either side of him must have been nearly ten stories tall.

Darren's slarm is going crazy. If he isn't careful, it'll take his face off. What good is it, really? The more he thinks about it, the more he thinks maybe it's some kind of signaling device for the other slags. How else would they have known they were all going to be there?

If he's going to have to look out for slags around every turn, he doesn't want to have to worry about one attached to his body. He roots through the nearest dumpster, filled with old trash beyond rotten, until he finds a tin can. It isn't a knife but it'll do. The lid is still attached to the can by about an inch of tin. He bends it up, holds the ridged part of the can, and begins hacking at his slarm at the shoulder, cutting on the slag part and not the Darren part. The slag gnashes its teeth and Darren angrily hacks at the front of it until the area approximating its mouth is loose and falling to the greasy asphalt. Then he continues hacking on the shoulder part. He doesn't feel any pain and when the slag is dangling there, Darren sticks his right hand into the gap and rips it the rest of the way off. Then he throws it on the ground and stomps it mercilessly. He turns to look at the end of the alley and sees Shell running.

He kind of wants Shell dead so he runs after him, wishing he had a gun or, fuck, even another arm would be great, at this point. Luckily, he still has the tin can clutched in his right hand.

16

Darren reaches the end of the alley and it occurs to him that, since Shell is running, he might be running *from* something. But it's too late. He turns to his left and sees an enormous slag half-running, half-slithering toward him. Its legs are too rudimentary to carry him quickly but they are there and Darren can only think about what they'll look like weeks or months from now.

Darren ducks back into the alleyway, knowing the slag has sensed him. The slag slows but doesn't stop completely and Darren thinks he is very lucky. Tentatively, he takes another step out of the alley. The slag is running off to his right, eclipsing Shell who runs before him. Darren thinks he could try and save Shell but he also thinks Shell is mostly the one who brought them here.

Where was Pearl?

Darren takes a deep breath and assesses things. Tries to orient himself and realizes it's impossible to orient yourself to someplace you've never been. What he needs to think about is getting out. Getting out or dying. Those are probably his only two choices. To his left two slags are battling each other. One is the older kind that looks like a slug except he's the size of a house. The other is the newer, more evolved kind, Tyrannosaurus rex-like arms and legs that, at this point, just jut out from the lower body, too small to even reach the ground.

The city is a patchwork of devastation. Some houses are destroyed while others are built up to three and four times their original sizes. Cars line the side of the road. Most of them are blackened shells. All of them are flattened. Trash and debris is strewn everywhere. Many things are on fire. The smoke and heat scorch his lungs and he wonders how much of what he is breathing is the nasty chemical stuff the Army used against the slags in the final days of the second attack. He realizes he doesn't care. It will just kill him quicker and, staring at the world he's left with, he thinks death is a very admirable option.

This world has probably long been scavenged and emptied of weapons by people who thought they had a chance at a time when that might have been true. A lengthy quest to find the perfect weapon is out of the question. He wishes he still had Gary. A blackened brick sits atop a pile of blackened bricks. He looks at the rusted can in his hand. Brick or can? He decides he can throw a brick. The can is too delicate to do damage if thrown. He drops the can and picks up the brick, turning to his right. Part of him wants to watch Shell get devoured by the slag.

Cautiously, he wanders down the broken sidewalk, looking through the shattered windows at sagging displays of merchandise finally revealed for what it is—worthless junk. To his left, hanging from an awning, are several dead bodies of varying shapes and sizes. They are all male and they have numbers tattooed onto their naked torsos. Maybe this had been a way to keep track of the dead at one point?

The slag is a couple blocks ahead of him and he can see it straining to force its way into one of those narrow alleys. It seems Shell had found a way to escape. That left him for Darren.

Darren doesn't know why he hates Shell so much. Perhaps it's his blind faith. If there were ever a thing to completely remove one's faith, Darren thought the apocalypse would surely be it.

Now how to get the slag away? Darren could always enter the building adjoining the alley and see if there was some kind of opening. Or he could just taunt the slag. Really tempt death.

He throws his brick at the hulking beast. It bounces off and clatters to the ground, breaking in half. Darren thinks about bending to pick it up but realizes he doesn't care. He's too tired. Instead, he just looks at the slag. And notices they are developing eyes. He doesn't know if this is a good or a bad thing. They seem to have done a fine job of sensing their prey. Now, with eyes, they would just be forced to look at the ugly world around them. Darren holds out his arms and waits for the slag to clamp down on him.

But it doesn't.

It snaps its giant teeth and Darren clenches his jaw thinking, *This is finally it.* But the slag is snapping its teeth at another slag, one that has slithered up behind Darren.

Darren steps out of the way.

Seeing the larger slag, the smaller one goes into some sort of frenzy and launches itself at the behemoth.

They're fighting each other.

That's why the large one was after Shell and didn't seem concerned with Darren. Shell still had the slag as a left arm. Darren had removed his. The slarms aren't weapons, they're bait.

He approaches the alley and turns to his right. Shell is huddled against a melted dumpster midway down the alley.

Darren approaches him slowly, wondering if Shell has a gun or not.

"How are you still alive?!" Shell yells. But it's not the authoritative yell he had used back in the chamber. It's a panicked yell. This is a different Shell, Darren thinks. One completely transformed by fear.

"Whose idea was the slarm?" Darren asks, moving closer and closer to Shell.

17

"Pearl's!" Shell shouts. And before Darren can stop him, he's jabbering on. "She's one of them. You don't understand. I don't know how I could have been so stupid. How I fell for it. I wasn't always like this. There was a time when I would never have fallen for something like this. She did something to me. She has powers. Do you know how important that is? Do you know how special it is to possess something like magic when it looks like the whole world is going to hell? Everybody was looking for something like that. Even people who didn't believe in anything wanted something to believe in because they knew they couldn't do it themselves. There was no way to survive on your own."

"I did."

"What?"

"I survived on my own. I did all of this on my own."

"You were ready to drown in the ocean."

"Better in the ocean than in the mouth of a slag."

Shell has no answer for that. Then he says, "I was here years ago. Before the second wave. All the residents believed that it was nearly slag free. They believed Pearl made it that way. They called her the Queen of Town. But you want to know what I think?"

"Not really."

"I think Pearl started the plague. I think there were no such things as slags. I think she found some way to come here through that goddamn fugue and bring her plague gods with her. And I think she had all the charm and magic to do it. Obviously."

"Obviously." Darren doesn't know whether or not to believe Shell. He supposes what he's saying is no more ludicrous than anything else he's witnessed over the past few days. He does believe Shell's intent is good and those good intentions may be what save Shell's life.

"What happened to your slarm?"

"Still haven't figured that one out, huh?"

Shell's one eye is blank. He isn't even able to draw his own conclusions.

"The slarm is a fucking signal. The slags don't want us anymore. It's probably been so long since they've eaten human they don't even remember we're food. They're eating themselves now. But they're also connected psychically or something. They can sense each other. Maybe it's sonar. By keeping that idiot thing on your shoulder, you're begging to be found and eaten. I bet Pearl knows where you are right now."

Shell's eye glazes over in fear.

"What do you think we should do?" Darren says.

"You're asking me? After I lead nearly twenty people to their deaths because I was too stupid to see the truth?"

"Well, there aren't really a lot of other people to ask. And I'm too tired to think. If it was up to me, I'd go out and lie in the street and beg for something to come along and either eat me or trample me to death."

"Get this thing off me!" Shell shouts and starts flapping the slarm.

Darren doesn't have the can anymore. He doesn't know how he's supposed to help him.

"I don't have any way to get it off," Darren says.

But Shell is already reaching down into his cargo pants. On the inside, not into a pocket. He brings out one of the largest knives Darren has ever seen. Then he starts hacking at the meat of his shoulder.

"You don't want to cut yourself," Darren says. "It won't bleed if you just cut the slag part."

Saying that doesn't do a lot of good. Shell continues hacking. It's like he went from crazy to bug fuck crazy in a matter of seconds.

"We have to find her," he spits, still hacking. "We have to find her and kill her. Take her out."

"You don't have to look for me."

Darren turns toward the entrance of the alley.

Pearl stands there in her summer dress. She's holding a gun, aiming it with both hands, and Darren thinks the gun could very well be Gary the Glock. She tightens up and fires. The roar is huge.

18

Shell's head erupts, the slarm only half off.

Darren quickly realizes he is in a whole lot of trouble. But, at this point, he feels like the proverbial tree in the forest. What if Pearl *is* one of them? What if *he* is the last human on earth? What then? Does he spend the rest of his days ejaculating into his own shit and trying to grow a homunculus? Does he just exist, fighting for survival every second? Our existence, he decides, is determined by those we coexist with. And he would try and find them. If he could make it through this, that's what he would have faith in. If people wanted to believe in ridiculous gods and anything with a touch of magic, then so be it. He would believe in his search. His quest. He would believe in his fellow humans, thinking more than just one must have survived.

Mainly, he wonders if Pearl has another shell in the gun.

He can run toward her or he can run away.

He runs away.

19

He runs away for the other side of the alley. Maybe then he'll have a second to think about what he can do because, at the moment, his options seem pretty damn limited.

And Pearl is standing directly in front of him. Blocking that side of the alley.

For a second, he thinks about turning around and going back to the other side of the alley but he sees this as a ridiculous game that could continue for hours. Unless she shoots him.

But she doesn't fire the gun. That might be a good sign.

Darren backs up until he steps in some of Shell's gore.

Pearl raises the gun and walks toward him.

He wishes he was attached to magical strings that could pull him up into the sky.

This is probably the end, he thinks. He has nothing. Nothing to defend himself with. The only person who can answer any of his questions is Pearl and he doesn't really think she'll tell him the truth.

She depresses the trigger and nothing happens.

Darren feels something close around his ankle. He looks down and sees Shell's head lift from the asphalt, leaving chunks behind. His one eye is vacant, zombified. He moves his head toward Darren's ankle and bites down.

From the other end of the alley, Pearl is laughing. She tosses the gun to the asphalt and begins walking toward him. Probably so she can feed on him. Darren kicks at Shell's head, looses his teeth from his flesh. Actually, it's more like his head just falls apart, the fractured skull unable to support it anymore.

He whips back around and Pearl is nearly on top of him. This close to him, he can see she isn't right. He doesn't know how Shell ever fell for it. Her skin is clearly slag skin, covered with a ton of make-up.

She lunges for him and he takes off running, nearly slipping in what's left of Shell. He waits for her to pop down on the other side of the alley but she doesn't. He turns to his left out on the sidewalk. He doesn't have any idea where he's going. He doesn't have any idea where to go. He just keeps running for two or three blocks. He loses count. It's impossible to keep track. And the blocks have been so destroyed and rearranged they do not give him any gauge of distance anyway.

Monstrous slags are all around him. Fighting amongst themselves. The larger slags eating the smaller slags.

Darren turns down another alley to his left. His lungs are burning and a vicious stitch has opened up in his side. What is he even running for?

He comes out on the other side of the alley. This street used to be lined with trees but now it's lined with charred stumps. He runs and expects to see Pearl at any moment. Now the street runs up hill and by the time he reaches the top his entire body is jelly.

But he sees something.

It looks like a dust storm. At the bottom of the hill. It's a swirling mass of something. He can't tell whether it's mist or dust. He figures this is probably the fugue they came through.

He stops at the top of the hill and looks down at it. Standing there, he can't tell if his muscles are too tired or if it's actually sucking at him, pulling him toward it.

All the slags in the area seem to be heading away from it. But maybe they're going slower than they were, also. He can't really tell. He wonders if he can go into the fugue and if it will take him someplace else. He wonders if this is exactly what Pearl wants. What would he find in there?

He knows what surrounds him and it is nothing but death and destruction. If there is any hope left it isn't in Hollow City.

He doesn't know what is in the fugue.

It could be life or death.

Slowly, he walks down the hill to meet it.

<h1 style="text-align:center">20</h1>

And he's sitting in a sun-filled kitchen back in his home in Indiana.

Lora, his wife, sits across the table from him.

Birds chirp outside. He can hear the boys playing in their room.

He feels a sense of doom.

"What?" Lora says.

"Hm?"

"You just got the funniest look on your face."

"I was just . . . thinking."

A newspaper sits in front of him and he picks it up with his right hand but when he goes to pull it open, it doesn't work. He looks at his missing left arm, his shirt all trussed up, and screams.

Lora is up and coming around the table to put her arm around his shoulders.

"It's okay," she says.

"How did I lose my arm!?" Darren barks.

"The war. You just . . . I can't talk about this again. Not right now."

Darren feels a burning in his chest, tries to reach back into his head and remember something but the only thing he finds is the smell of burning flesh.

Lora opens a cabinet door and says, "Here. Take one of these. It'll make you feel better."

She hands Darren an oblong white pill.

She turns her back to run a glass of water at the sink.

She puts the glass on the table in front of Darren.

"Go on," she says. "Take it. If you don't take it, you'll start screaming . . . And that scares the boys."

Darren throws the pill in his mouth and swallows the water, keeping the pill between his teeth and gums. He stands up and says, "I'm gonna go outside for a bit."

"There," Lora says. "Better already."

He walks out the back door and spits the pill out into the grass. As soon as he put it in his mouth, his sense of doom increased. He doesn't see how that could possibly make him feel any better.

To swallow the pill would be to forget everything. To swallow the pill would mean staying right where he was and disintegrating along with it because this place, it isn't real.

Darren goes out to the garage and rummages around until he finds his Glock. He checks to make sure the clip is full and shoves it back in the grip. It makes a satisfying click. He wonders how real it is.

He walks out of the garage and toward the house. The house looks different. It looks rundown. There are holes in the walls, the siding. He can see right through it. He puts his hand on the door handle and pulls. It nearly falls off its hinges. It reminds him of paper. He walks through the house until he comes to the boys' room. He pulls the door open. Lora is in there with them. They all look at him.

He fires three shots.

21

And watches his family disintegrate into three piles of slags that quickly wriggle together to form one vaguely human-like mass.

Darren looks at his gun, slightly amazed it actually fired.

He aims it at the slag mass and fires again.

Nothing. Even though he knows the clip is full. But he knows the paper thinness of this world extends to everything, not just the walls of his house.

The mass walks toward him. Darren fires the gun again to no avail. He throws the gun at the mass of slags in one last pitiful attempt to stave them off. He sinks to his knees and raises his arm, baring his throat and his heart. The mass sickeningly sloshes toward him. He hears a high-pitched buzzing to his right, drawing closer, louder. He turns his head to the right but whatever is making the buzzing sound is a blur. Something clamps onto his arm and yanks him to the left, nearly ripping the arm out of its socket.

A voice yells, "*Deus ex machina!*"

Now Darren is being dragged from his crumbling paper house and doesn't come to rest until they reach the real world, the devastated world destroyed by slags.

Finally, he is able to open his eyes and look at his rescuer. He sits atop an old dirt bike, holding out his hand.

"I'm Kid Rider, fuckmunch."

"Thanks," he chokes out and takes the Kid's hand. He stands up.

"We ain't done yet." Kid Rider points back toward the fugue.

Pearl is at the edge of the fugue. There's an opening there. Darren thinks of a vagina. Pearl is sewing it up. Rather, it looks like she had begun sewing it up but now she is crossing the expanse between them, carrying a huge gleaming needle.

"She was tryin' to sew it up so we'd be stuck in there," Kid Rider says. "Look out!"

Darren ducks just as a massive slag chomps down behind him. The mouth opens again and Kid Rider throws something down its gullet. The slag lurches, vomits up something that smells really foul and collapses onto the ground.

Darren takes the brief opportunity to scan his surroundings. The slags are devouring each other. They don't seem to be the least bit interested in him and Kid Rider. Everything organic looks like it has already been eaten.

Darren whips back around. Kid Rider pulls an extremely nefarious-looking machine gun from the side of his dirt bike.

"Back off, Pearl." He hoists the machine gun up until the butt rests against his shoulder. Before he can even squeeze off a round, Pearl throws the needle at the gun. It lodges in the barrel and Kid Rider manages to hold off squeezing the trigger. Darren doesn't know what would have happened. Pearl lets out a scream and throws herself at Kid Rider, knocking him from the bike. The machine gun goes flying. Darren figures it's useless so he throws himself on Pearl, wrapping an arm around her neck and trying to pull her from Kid Rider. She tosses him off easily and says, "This isn't between me and you."

But Darren thinks it kind of is. Up until he had met Pearl, his life had seemed easy. Kid Rider manages to kick her off. Darren grabs the machine gun. He tries to pull the needle out but it won't budge. Pearl fakes a charge at Kid Rider and then turns abruptly and runs for the dirt bike. Kid Rider is running after her.

"Stop her! Stop her!" he shouts.

Darren hoists the gun up with his one good arm. He'll never be able to keep it steady. He wonders if the bullets will come out the stock end, severing his other arm. He doesn't care.

"Move!" Darren shouts at Kid Rider. Kid Rider drops to the ground and rolls to his right.

Darren aims at the ground just behind the dirt bike and squeezes the trigger. A few shots blast out. Most of them sail high into the air.

But one of them hits the dirt bike. It swerves crazily and dumps Pearl to the ground.

"Finish it! Finish it!" Kid Rider shouts.

"I can't aim," Darren says and throws the gun toward the Kid. He quickly grabs it up and charges toward the rising Pearl. She's lightning quick, standing up and charging for the fugue. Kid Rider fires the machine gun, drilling Pearl in the back.

But it doesn't stop her from entering the fugue.

Then the fugue collapses into itself like a balloon made of dust.

Darren and Kid Rider stand staring at it.

22

"Did you kill her?" Darren asks.

"Don't know. Them bullets was packed with slag repellant. It'd kill a normal slag but I don't know about her."

"How will we know?"

"If the other slags start dying, then I'd reckon she was dead."

"And if not?"

"We're probably fucked."

"I think we're fucked anyway."

"Why do you say that?"

"Well, I haven't seen any humans for quite a while and, seeing as we both have penises, this might be it."

Kid Rider looked down at the ground. "Speak for yourself," he said. "I've got a big ol' vagina and I probably got all the girl organs too."

Darren looks at him.

"Yeah, I know I ain't real attractive but you only got one arm. Like a slot machine. I'll call you Slotty."

"I didn't say anything."

"Yeah, but you was thinkin' it."

The Kid pulls up the dirt bike and hops on. He motions to the back and says, "Hop on. You get to be the bitch. We're gonna do things right this time."

Darren, at a complete loss for words, hops on. The Kid fires up the dirt bike and they go buzzing down the road. The slags continue gnawing on one another and Kid Rider tells him he knows a real good place where they can hide. They pass through the flaming ruins of the city, ready to wait it out.

Other Grindhouse Press Titles

#666__*Satanic Summer* by Andersen Prunty
#106__*Depraved Halloween* by Bryan Smith
#105__*Dread Ink* by Bryan Smith
#104__*Jack and Mr. Grin* by Andersen Prunty
#103__*What Ever Happened to Jo Rose?* by Chris DiLeo
#102__*I Think I'm Alone Now* by Ali Seay
#101__*Cute Aggression* by Emily Lynn
#100__*Headless* by Scott Cole
#099__*The Killing Kind* by Bryan Smith
#098__*An Affinity for Formaldehyde* by Chloe Spencer
#097__*Kill The Hunter* by Bryan Smith
#096__*The Gauntlet* by Bryan Smith
#095__*Bad Movie Night* by Patrick Lacey
#094__*Hysteria: Lolly & Lady Vanity* by Ali Seay
#093__*The Prettiest Girl in the Grave* by Kristopher Triana
#092__*Dead End House* by Bryan Smith
#091__*Graffiti Tombs* by Matt Serafini
#090__*The Hands of Onan* by Chris DiLeo
#089__*Burning Down the Night* by Bryan Smith
#088__*Kill Hill Carnage* by Tim Meyer
#087__*Meat Photo* by C.V. Hunt and Andersen Prunty
#086__*Dreaditation* by Andersen Prunty
#085__*The Unseen II* by Bryan Smith
#084__*Waif* by Samantha Kolesnik
#083__*Racing with the Devil* by Bryan Smith
#082__*Bodies Wrapped in Plastic and Other Items of Interest*
        by Andersen Prunty
#081__*The Next Time You See Me I'll Probably Be Dead* by C.V. Hunt
#080__*The Unseen* by Bryan Smith
#079__*The Late Night Horror Show* by Bryan Smith
#078__*Birth of a Monster* by A.S. Coomer
#077__*Invitation to Death* by Bryan Smith
#076__*Paradise Club* by Tim Meyer
#075__*Mage of the Hellmouth* by John Wayne Comunale
#074__*The Rotting Within* by Matt Kurtz
#073__*Go Down Hard* by Ali Seay
#072__*Girl of Prey* by Pete Risley
#071__*Gone to See the River Man* by Kristopher Triana

#070__*Horrorama* edited by C.V. Hunt

#069__*Depraved 4* by Bryan Smith

#068__*Worst Laid Plans: An Anthology of Vacation Horror* edited by
      Samantha Kolesnik

#067__*Deathripping: Collected Horror Stories* by Andersen Prunty

#066__*Depraved* by Bryan Smith

#065__*Crazytimes* by Scott Cole

#064__*Blood Relations* by Kristopher Triana

#063__*The Perfectly Fine House* by Stephen Kozeniewski
      and Wile E. Young

#062__*Savage Mountain* by John Quick

#061__*Cocksucker* by Lucas Milliron

#060__*Luciferin* by J. Peter W.

#059__*The Fucking Zombie Apocalypse* by Bryan Smith

#058__*True Crime* by Samantha Kolesnik

#057__*The Cycle* by John Wayne Comunale

#056__*A Voice So Soft* by Patrick Lacey

#055__*Merciless* by Bryan Smith

#054__*The Long Shadows of October* by Kristopher Triana

#053__*House of Blood* by Bryan Smith

#052__*The Freakshow* by Bryan Smith

#051__*Dirty Rotten Hippies and Other Stories* by Bryan Smith

#050__*Rites of Extinction* by Matt Serafini

#049__*Saint Sadist* by Lucas Mangum

#048__*Neon Dies At Dawn* by Andersen Prunty

#047__*Halloween Fiend* by C.V. Hunt

#046__*Limbs: A Love Story* by Tim Meyer

#045__*As Seen On T.V.* by John Wayne Comunale

#044__*Where Stars Won't Shine* by Patrick Lacey

#043__*Kinfolk* by Matt Kurtz

#042__*Kill For Satan!* by Bryan Smith

#041__*Dead Stripper Storage* by Bryan Smith

#040__*Triple Axe* by Scott Cole

#039__*Scummer* by John Wayne Comunale

#038__*Cockblock* by C.V. Hunt

#037__*Irrationalia* by Andersen Prunty

#036__*Full Brutal* by Kristopher Triana

#035__*Office Mutant* by Pete Risley

#034__*Death Pacts and Left-Hand Paths* by John Wayne Comunale

#033__*Home Is Where the Horror Is* by C.V. Hunt

#032__*This Town Needs A Monster* by Andersen Prunty

#031__*The Fetishists* by A.S. Coomer

#030__*Ritualistic Human Sacrifice* by C.V. Hunt

#029__*The Atrocity Vendor* by Nick Cato

#028__*Burn Down the House and Everyone In It* by Zachary T. Owen

#027__*Misery and Death and Everything Depressing* by C.V. Hunt

#026__*Naked Friends* by Justin Grimbol

#025__*Ghost Chant* by Gina Ranalli

#024__*Hearers of the Constant Hum* by William Pauley III

#023__*Hell's Waiting Room* by C.V. Hunt

#022__*Creep House: Horror Stories* by Andersen Prunty

#021__*Other People's Shit* by C.V. Hunt

#020__*The Party Lords* by Justin Grimbol

#019__*Sociopaths In Love* by Andersen Prunty

#018__*The Last Porno Theater* by Nick Cato

#017__*Zombieville* by C.V. Hunt

#016__*Samurai Vs. Robo-Dick* by Steve Lowe

#015__*The Warm Glow of Happy Homes* by Andersen Prunty

#014__*How To Kill Yourself* by C.V. Hunt

#013__*Bury the Children in the Yard: Horror Stories*
   by Andersen Prunty

#012__*Return to Devil Town (Vampires in Devil Town Book Three)*
   by Wayne Hixon

#011__*Pray You Die Alone: Horror Stories* by Andersen Prunty

#010__*King of the Perverts* by Steve Lowe

#009__*Sunruined: Horror Stories* by Andersen Prunty

#008__*Bright Black Moon (Vampires in Devil Town Book Two)*
   by Wayne Hixon

#007__*Hi I'm a Social Disease: Horror Stories* by Andersen Prunty

#006__*A Life On Fire* by Chris Bowsman

#005__*The Sorrow King* by Andersen Prunty

#004__*The Brothers Crunk* by William Pauley III

#003__*The Horribles* by Nathaniel Lambert

#002__*Vampires in Devil Town* by Wayne Hixon

#001__*House of Fallen Trees* by Gina Ranalli

#000__*Morning is Dead* by Andersen Prunty